BOOK BIN BABY

Book Bin Baby

A novel
by

LAZAR SARNA

Adelaide Books
New York / Lisbon
2020

BOOK BIN BABY
A novel
By Lazar Sarna

Copyright © by Lazar Sarna
Cover design © 2020 Adelaide Books

Published by Adelaide Books, New York / Lisbon
adelaidebooks.org
Editor-in-Chief
Stevan V. Nikolic

For any information, please address Adelaide Books
at info@adelaidebooks.org
or write to:
Adelaide Books
244 Fifth Ave. Suite D27
New York, NY, 10001

ISBN: 978-1-951896-35-5

Printed in the United States of America

To my Jewel, whose perception of life matches mine.

Contents

Chapter 1

Shopping Interrupted

He was born in the book bin in the Library.

Obsessed with finding the lowest price on household items, his mother Napanee, on her due date, in the throes of a shopping mission, ran outside the kitchen-accessories outlet looking for a safe place to hatch, waddled into the Mortimer Ketchum Library next door, pulled the baby from between her legs, placed him on her two-for-one bath towels in the return book bin for soft children's books only, and scurried back to the all-gadgets-on-sale sale.

Music sprayed like fine mist out the ceiling loud-speakers. A medley of Gershwin tunes was reset to capture the spirit of 1975. Gershwin was interrupted by an understated announcement beckoning the maintenance man to Towels to 'visit' a spill in aisle six where her water had broken. Napanee had already moved onto the appliances to see the price of battery-powered beaters.

She knew her baby would be safe where she had left him because there was little or no activity. Had she liked Gershwin, she would have called her baby George or Gershwin. Had she thought the brothers Ira and George were rivals, she might have picked George, simply to take sides. Instead, she called him Price when she noticed two different prices stamped on the tag attached to a toaster oven. If Price were to have a brother, to which Napanee would never agree to, his name, like her own, would be reminiscent of a foreign culture, something British like a brand of upper-end furniture.

"What's wrong with you, belly," she talked openly. "Don't like being empty? Welcome to becoming flat, like it used to be."

She leaned her elbows on the shopping cart handlebar, wishing the waves of dizziness would stop, until they did. Napanee pressed more hand towels into her maternity pants.

The miracle of permanent press and stain resistance could not be denied or suppressed. Of course she was proud of her clothing. Her feelings went beyond pride. Her clothing stood by her under duress. They exemplified staunch faith, self-sacrifice and loyalty from the waistbands to colour resilience, to smart fit and shape. She nodded to them, acknowledged their service to the cause of her body.

It was by pure instinct of the species that Napanee felt giving a child a name was more valuable than giving him milk. Price not only identified him: it connected the baby with her self and caused her rapture. She did not have the opportunity to call him by his new name for several days because she was caught up in the grand opening of a depot store miles north of the Library. Door-crashers, blow-outs and three-for-one items made it humanly impossible to return to her business of first-time mother until the bargains exhausted themselves.

"How many miniature TV sets do I really need," she complained to her mother on the phone, who took the occasion to remind her to look for pewter accent pieces for the dining room.

"I couldn't get to them. My water broke and I had to drop off the baby. By the time I came back..."

Her mother was too busy assembling her thoughts. "Maybe they give rainy day coupons. If I were you..."

"I am not you. You know enough to trust me. So trust me."

"You'll do your best. Everyone wants to take advantage of us. How is your tummy? If you're too tired, sit down near the check-out so the girls will recognize you and let you in on the lines later on."

Her mother forgot to ask what Napanee was wearing. When she was in the process of giving practical advice, she considered outfitting to be secondary. In her mind that day, her mother assumed Napanee was sporting her jean jumper with the generous pockets that detracted from her belly. That worried her because it gave no coverage to the growing hints of flab in her upper arms, unless she brought her decorative neck-scarf with her.

Shopping was an alternative geography. In that realm, two prices on one item was a discordant event, an eclipse or violent earthquake. Napanee, like a reporter for an exploration magazine, knew that mounds of merchandise hid something archeologically telling. The voice over the loudspeakers announcing a newly minted price reduction in the corner of the store was the same voice proclaiming revelation to Graham Bell that the telephone worked or that Tutenkhamen had been discovered. The store even had its own weather: no clouds, no rain, no frost nor volcanoes that could end its existence.

In this geography, Harry Souply her husband, who abandoned her in the second month of her pregnancy, was now no more appealing than returned goods in a torn plastic bag. Harry was less than a villain because his advent and disappearance made no profound impression on her behavior. He was a familiar passenger on a train, recognizable by his presence, inconsequential in his absence. He hunted other business opportunities and perhaps other women for excitement while she was left alone to perform the task no-one else was capable of loving: selecting from the mass of product produced by the nation what was needed for the home and person at a price closest to cost. It was more than a hunt: it was the natural way to evacuate energy, convert it into what many critics call a life's work.

The maintenance man found a fetid puddle near the gadget display, which he immediately removed. They told him to go to Towels; he used his own initiative to find the offending problem around the aisle. Although no-one was going to credit him for his extra expenditure of energy, he did file a grievance with Human Resources because he was being assigned imprecise jobsites. His job was to restore the status quo ante, not locate it.

Nothing in the store was there by accident. Any accident did not belong on the shelf or the floor because it had no place in the system. The floor was purely functional, a pathway through the forest of goods. The shelving bore the fruit of the forest, arranged not by whim of nature but by accessibility and preference. An accident was not a fruit in the forest.

"No one knows anything," he would lament.

He could not figure out what he had found. That did not bother him because he had not been hired to do a pathology report. His report sheet required a tick mark next to damaged merchandise, human liquids or toxic materials. It was too troublesome to record anything but human liquids: otherwise he would have to detail in another report what he did with the damaged merchandise or toxic materials.

The manager was always concerned this man thought too much. An electrician once commented he was like the ideal Marxian worker who philosophized.

"You know, do your work and that's the end of it. If you thought about everything, nothing would get done."

He had a warped view of who the truly essential workers in the system were: maintenance people and store detectives. They were the permanent scavengers scouring the terrain. Cashiers, inventory controllers, refund clerks and store designers were replaceable birds of passage. The problem with detectives was the age-old one: who polices the police? Maintenance, on the other hand, was open to everyone's appreciation and criticism. Those who cleaned up were, by definition, fearless. Fearless enough to say to the dispatcher that she had sent him to the wrong place, and if she were going to continue doing that, she might as well clean it up herself.

Napanee trusted the ecosystem of commerce and human intrigue. While it may not have been secure against shoplifting and the occasional armed robbery, those were matters for the cashiers and executives. On the floor, she was as safe as home; at home as much as home, where the business of staying open guaranteed she was always welcome.

The Mortimer Ketchum reference librarian, the all-purpose man who had just reinforced one of the shelves, and a Library governor all milled about and ogled the baby, running with tissue or towels from the 24-hour pharmacy to tamp it and provide it comfort. The all-purpose man picked it up and put it down. What a novel way, the governor thought, to attract new members. Maybe a nanny at minimum wage could be found to make the baby fresh every little while, feed it and keep it comfortable. Perhaps one of the girls of the woman who dusted and did the floors. As it turned out, the duster agreed to look after the baby's needs during working hours. Sometimes, she brought in her daughter's baby to play in the same bin.

She cleaned the bin of dust as best she could. It was impossible to get the bits of dust and paper out of the cracks. The babies were not aware of each other's presence. They knew each other as an obstruction, or a poke in the eye, or an upsetting wail. Certainly they smelt each other and pressed each other's pudge. They had no need to explain themselves nor prophesize they would be living in two distinct worlds.

New sales arose and continued for days, then weeks at the nearby outlets. Each morning, Napanee returned with a list of things to buy for herself and friends. She would visit the baby on her rounds and get some air. She left it a card on which she had written, 'My name is Price.' A gaggle of Library moms and their tots brought warm milk, pieces of donut, diapers. Napanee was glad those were good educated hands touching Price. Since the Library closed at six most evenings, and lights dimmed at six-thirty, Price would fall into a good sleep routine.

At night, the Library rested. It exhaled one big breath after the ebb and flow of the book trade of the day. It grew smaller, maybe curling up within itself, huddling its atlases and magazines. All the wild, somber, novel, decaying, angry, turbulent, childish, logical and imitative ideas, characters, plots, hypotheses and firm conclusions squashed into all the books grew as silent as a fly's carcass in the winter. Night was not death; it was a truce. What a place to be if you were a baby, Napanee thought in a glow. A baby has needs reduceable to warmth. It sleeps in visions of colour and fuzzy ideas.

Little did she know the violence that expressed itself in the hour after closing. The clean-up girl muttered curses to the world as she picked up books, straightened volumes on the shelf and emptied trash. Price could see her pile up books on the floor, divide them into categories of smaller piles, push them selectively into the stacks, all the while working her jaw as if chewing something constantly re-visiting from her stomach. Over and over, she made piles, stood the books with spines up, filed and chewed with brisk, pre-meditated assertive movements. It was the rhythm that smoothed his way to sleep.

The same rhythm confirmed his baby belief in resurrection. The knowledge he had of his recent creation, and the constant stacking of books, aided by the repetitious taping of torn pages into volumes by the staff during the day, demonstrated the cyclical direction of life. He was just a shelved book, later to become unshelved and finally reshelved. The day he discovered his thumb was the day he concluded that progress followed a path of novelty, which later must be followed by boredom with novelty, regression, and ultimately rebirth.

This was no different than the activity of the girls on the floor at the stores after hours; yet Napanee felt the Library would set appropriate ethical standards for the growing infant during the day. The posters conveyed life's mission and spoke of pride in being part of the community, of earning trust, being friendly, and seeking new members. Napanee especially wanted the baby to know the motto that would not change for years: *Make our Library your Home.* Here, home was pronounced by the junior members with a long decadent "m", so that the word could defectively rhyme with "warm". Most current poets abandoned rhyme as a creative device because it became too corny for the starkness of their ideas. This motto, however, was firmly rooted in tradition.

"I want you to tell me if he needs anything," she told one of the volunteers.

"What does he need?" she asked.

"Probably nothing. Every time I drop in he looks so happy. I wonder how he gets dressed," she said to the air.

"Are you the mother?"

"Who do you think I am, a past-due clerk?"

Napanee had never frequented the stores as much as she had following the birth of Price. Several times a day, she called her mother about the bargains she had found and the incessant attention the droves of Library members were paying to the baby. Her mother became alarmed for the wrong reason: she implored her to get a job at one of the stores so she could receive an employee's discount on purchases, which is what she did. The fact that Price was being exposed to a multitude of germs and unscreened strangers was not even an issue: it was a distraction. It was like having a meaningful discussion on the growth of western nationalism, only to have your discussion partner interrupt with a display of family vacation pictures.

"If you're going to spend so much time there, you might as well get paid for it", she said with a nag.

Napanee and her mother spoke twice in the morning, twice in the afternoon, and all evening. This was a routine they had established since Napanee had left high school. Fair to say their talk was largely inconsequential; but so is a monkey's nit-picking of a fellow's fur. They talked to hear that mother was there and child was there. She was wrapping it in a parental blanket.

"I was so excited today, I ran out of quarters", Napanee told her one evening after getting a three hundred dollar reduction on a fridge because of a scratch on the side.

"I think you'd be good as a price checker. You know, no more double amounts", her mother counseled.

"Did I tell you? I called the baby Price", Napanee said with pride. Giving birth to a child was an unavoidable mess. Giving it a name, however, was a craft, like the final act of setting a diamond.

Her mother was silent for a moment. She needed the time to formulate an adage she had heard before. None was forthcoming.

"There's no point in telling your mother good news if it's already old. I want to be the first to know. Who did you tell?" Her maternal pride was being tested.

"No one knows except me and the baby. And now I'm talking to the grandmother."

"A boy? The baby's a boy? Don't tell me he looks like..." her mother sighed uncomfortably. Ironically, she was the one who spurred her daughter on to marry Harry as quickly as possible.

"I think he looks like Harry. But I haven't been able to take a really good look at him... I don't think Harry knows anything since he disappeared." Napanee had not spoken his name until now. Since he left, she either referred to him by pronoun or thought minimally of him by vague form of face.

"Your husband doesn't know and doesn't care. Your father's trying to track him down. Put him in jail for the way he treated you," Napanee's mother said.

She had assumed the burden of molding Harry into a source of pain, of taking that pain from her daughter and firing up her husband to do the practical thing. It was easy because Napanee's mother internalized nothing. She had no repository of unspoken grudges, urges, desires or despairs because she said everything she felt on the spot.

Unlike Napanee, peace came to her mother easily, as did sleep. She fell asleep while swimming in the middle of a lake, her natural buoyancy flipping her body on its back while she dreamt. Driving more than ten minutes was so tranquilizing, she had to pull over to close her eyes. When she was jolted by some discordance, large or minuscule, she would let out a sudden "Oh", frightening family members while she chopped carrots, even though what provoked her was the sudden remembrance of a hairdresser's appointment the next day. Like Napanee, when she gave birth, her thoughts were elsewhere.

"There was something I was supposed to do today, and now I can't remember what it is, and I can't do it anyway."

The name Napanee came to her in a black-and-white dream about back-packing in the far North and encountering Indians who were selling beads and milk-shake mixers for next to nothing.

In order to convey the seriousness of a conversation he would initiate, her husband Gerald summoned up a serious face by puffing out his lips and staring over her head. He knew he would have to speak quickly before her attention drifted into something she thought might also be serious. She often recalled how she slept in the lake and awoke in an invisible bed of water, much the same way fish must sleep.

"Our daughter gave birth?" he asked for confirmation.

"Didn't you hear me talking on the phone with Napanee?" his wife answered.

"I'm not supposed to pick it up out of your telephone conversations. You're supposed to tell me to my face."

"Now it's old news. Next time you'll be the first to know when I find out."

"If you remember."

"Then you'll remind me."

Napanee was twenty-three. The only thing she had never done in all that time was work. Earning money meant asking her father for it.

"I hate asking you for money. Why don't you just leave it in the empty fish-bowl, or in the Perry Como record jacket?"

"Someone might take it."

"Who's going to take it?"

Working as a price checker at the warehouse store, though, was an interesting proposition. Someone called a boss would give orders and pay salary. Maybe she and the boss could go out to lunch every Monday to get a jump on the week. The boss would either be in a suit, or wear a short-sleeved shirt and wear a company hat.

She would tell him: "Think of me as a customer working the other side. I think like a customer so I can take her on. Why don't we give out free mints at the cash while people wait? Why don't we always have a 5-for-1 sale?"

Her father admired her for only one reason: Napanee was able to return purchases and act as if she had a right to do so. She could return opened bottles of wine to the store, stereo equipment she had scratched while moving from room to room, and partially-eaten restaurant food. She succeeded where he had failed all his life. As a boy, his mother had him buy a pound of cottage cheese from the grocer. He would bring it home wrapped in wet waxed paper, shoved into a crumbling paper bag. His mother would taste a few crumbs, declare it was not fresh, and order him to return it for a re-fund. How many times did the grocer berate his sheepish face when he came back to the store with the puddle of cheese? How many times did he wish he lived on another planet? Until he finally took action: when his mother sent him off to buy the cheese, he came back empty-handed, breaking the sad news that the grocer did not have any, or that it did not smell fresh.

"I told him my mother doesn't want old stuff. And it looks green."

At those times when he did buy and was sent back, he simply threw the cheese at the neighborhood cats and told his mother he used the refund money to buy chocolate milk and an apple which he had consumed. He could not understand why his mother constantly ordered and rarely kept it. No-one in the house ate it even if, on rare occasions, the cheese was good enough to reach his icebox. This is why he hated Harry until Gerald's death. Harry was a piece of cheese, a sad lump of curdled milk in soggy paper, with its own reason for being, a reason only hungry cats might understand.

"Do you understand Harry that I have no feelings toward you?"

Harry told him it was natural for a father-in-law to feel that way.

"How would you know that?"

"My friends tell me."

"How many of your friends have fathers-in-law, Harry?"

"Uh… none of them. They're not married yet."

Napanee was this-worldly. Unless an object had an appraisable value, it did not exist. An idea did not exist unless it was an accessory to an object. If she were introduced to the Unfinished Symphony, she might wonder if it were like an unfinished toaster. Was it cheaper if unfinished or could it be repackaged as something else, like a finished concerto, to be made more marketable?

This did not mean she was crude or intellectually incapable. She had a focused interest which defined her patience. No interest, no patience: not an unusual motto to live by. If she spoke about the bargain on school supplies, her conversation could not be diverted to another subject until each facet of trigonometry sets and three-hole punched loose-leaf had been ventilated. Napanee was thorough to a degree absurd to anyone who could not care less about her conversational obsession. That made her absurd to many and admirable to her father. On family road trips, she would not let Gerald stop for gas until she was satisfied the price of super had reached its lowest level. She left the decision on whether or not to marry Harry to her parents because she had no patience to deal with it.

"Don't you think when you go places, it's nice to say, this is my husband," her mother said.

"Not if I have to drag him everywhere," Napanee countered.

"Everyone I know drags husbands."

Gerald intervened: "Marry him, I don't like him. Maybe that's because I'm your father. You marry him. He's your problem. I don't have to like him for you to deal with him."

The decision to have Price was not pre-meditated, and for that reason, was not a decision. At first she thought of her pregnancy as a growth, in the same way an x-ray film thinks of white blobs in lung tissue. Having adjusted to the idea, she just let it grow because she had other things to work on.

Having a first baby was not a seminal event. Something else had radically changed her life. Napanee came late in life to blondness. Her brunette had gone blond at age seventeen. Wherever she entered, whether a room, a closet, a car, an outdoor patio, she felt her aura of blondness preceded her, as if her hair and bleached eyebrows were a magnificent flashlight or halo of radiance, accompanied by the chord of a choir.

Napanee had an inkling that historically, blondness was associated with the smell of bleach, which is what she fervently strove to avoid. For that reason, she refused to enter any beauty salon that smelled of bleach, in the same way she refused to visit any relative or acquaintance in a seniors' residence or hospital room that had any lingering scent of urine. Archeological digs in Troy, Babylonia and Central Europe uncovered vials of bleach which were at first attributed to the cotton and wool manufacturing process and later attributed to cosmetics, especially since they were found among combs and face paints. She enjoyed being part of the cosmetic movement in history, the process working itself out in the temples and curls of those who knew its value.

Napanee was now complete. She had been through the cycle of her own birth and development, and had given birth. She had been born with blonde highlights that faded into a thick brunette. Again, she carried on the cycle to see her hair golden like wheat fields. She was a fancy Mother Earth, a blonde field of radiance waving to the matching blue sky, colours never changing until the fashion season ineluctably came to a close. And Price was blonde.

Chapter 2

Library Is Happy

The main problem in building the Library was accommodating the Ketchum bequest that the structure should *"evoke
the memory of the great ship Titanic so that by merely looking at
its exterior, passersby would immediately recall the tragedy."* The
trustees had the architect, the brother-in-law of one of them,
and who promised reasonably low fees, create a series of con-
ceptual drawings, all of which were voted down. One drawing
depicted a ship made of red brick, port holes, and only one
smoke stack. Others showed a square, squat structure, with
bow and stern projecting from opposite sides, or a façade of
decks with people wearing navy outfits waving handkerchiefs.
The most arresting concept displayed the boat stood up on its
stern as if about to sink, doors and port holes on the bottom
of the hull.

"I have never put so much emotion into a concept," the
architect said with a tremble as he discussed the flow of lines
and melding of forms.

"Not enough room left in it for taste," one Trustee said.

"Volumes have been written on what constitutes taste," he rebutted.

"I know what sits well in my stomach."

"Am I talking to a group of stomachs, then?"

The first drawing submitted by the new architect replacing the brother-in-law who still insisted on being paid for his labour, won everyone's endearment. The structure would be standard library vintage, two-storeyed, brick and granite façade, wide sweep of exterior stairs leading up to columns guarding the front doors. In front, a wide shallow reflecting pool fed by a fountain, whose base was engraved with the words: *"In memory of the Titanic"*. In winter, the pool was to serve as a skating rink. It was built according to specification, except for the spelling of the ship, which had two *T*s in the middle of its name.

For a small library, it proved to be an ongoing source of interest and controversy. Even in its later years, when it was surrounded by commercial buildings, it became a much sought-after development site. Head librarians came and went as they tried unsuccessfully to liven up the services offered beyond a mere repository of books. The coffee-house evenings featuring young Yale Poetry Series authors had to close because someone snuck in unlicensed alcohol, and because of window-smashing of neighbouring storefronts. A fashion show caused a police raid when one middle-aged model appeared topless from a distance, when in fact she was wearing a flesh-toned, tight jersey. Each time a science fair was held, there was either an explosion, or fire, or irrepressible stench. The trustees were so sensitive to untoward attention the librarians paid with their jobs if a controversial event occurred on their watch.

A social services inspector came to see the baby five days after Napanee was hired as a price checker. She wore a business suit, only one sleeve of which was densely wrinkled. Her stiletto heels increased her maneuverability on her toes. She admired the fact that Napanee had her child near work but strongly recommended it not be kept in the book bin without supervision. The inspector was mindful of an old rule at the office: never practice social work in a commercial section of the city. Yet she cared enough to tell the people in charge; "Don't make me come back." She gave out her business cards which had an inked-in correction to the telephone and fax numbers. The head librarian was not eager to change one of the biggest draws he had in years. He was the one who mollified social services by installing bumpers and a guard rail around the bin to prevent injury to the infant.

"It's part of the way we look after our family", he told a reporter for the give-away newspaper distributed at all of the factory outlets. "As far as we're concerned, Price can live here as long as he wants to."

The Library board was meeting every ten days on the subject. Prior to Price's advent, board members only saw each other at a meeting once a year. The president was beaming at the most recent meeting.

"Miracles happen. This institution was dying until a little baby floated down from heaven. Membership is up five-fold. Our chief librarian has made sure that anyone who now enters the building just to see the baby, has to be a member, and he signs him up if he isn't. Last year I told you my biggest concern was illiteracy. The fact that several of you still say 'liberry' used to bother me. I don't care anymore. We are now getting national prominence."

After the meeting, the President was arrested on a nuisance charge at the bank. He refused to leave the teller's station until she said "cash" instead of "cesh". No one else in the line seemed to mind how the teller spoke English as long as she dispensed money.

Mortimer Ketchum made his money by not spending most of it. He and his wife Mary lived in a mansion on the hill above the small bridge. They never entertained and had only one domestic helper. Delivery men had to leave their packages at the doorstep. The door was never opened for anyone at night, even the doctor. Mr. Ketchum, in mid-life, had invented sliding rails for processing equipment shunts, bringing him enormous royalties for the rest of his lifetime and beyond. The couple never had any children, never wanted any themselves and had no need for any social life or niceties as long as they had each other. Mary Ketchum acted as his secretary at the office he maintained in town. Beyond interaction with business people during the day, they saw no reason to bring anyone home. They were not articulate, were mistakenly thought to be curt and rude. They had no interest in religion or partying, and were considered to be stoics or hermits.

It came as a surprise that he left his money to the founding of a public library. His will spoke lovingly of children and the need to brighten their minds through books. He so loved his bath tub, he instructed it be placed in the Library.

The bust of Mortimer Ketchum was fashioned posthumously from two stark passport photos. Although Mortimer and Mary cut each other's hair out of distrust for barbers, the sculptor chose not to reproduce his off-kilter part and longish strands of hair, tangled eyebrows and cheek bones free of a bad beard. The portrait of Mary depicted a background of books even though there were only two books in the mansion, an old almanac and a recipe collection. Their reading room had been filled with wide piles of newspapers which occasionally smoldered from spontaneous combustion.

Had Napanee traveled generations backward to appear on their doorstep, she would not have knocked, and the Ketchums would not have answered. Had she had a baby in her arms, they would have looked through the windows toward the porch and hidden below the sash.

Mr. Ketchum had a house next to his mansion he called the bird house. It was built as the servant's quarters but no servant wanted to or did live in it. The owner left food for neighborhood birds on the window sills, hoping to invite them in through an open door. At its peak, one hundred birds flew around its rooms. Every half hour, Mr. Ketchum had a local boy walk around banging two pots together to get the jays and sparrows circulating. The trick seemed to work; no birds roosted, and while there were feathers and down scattered on the floors, there was little dirt. The pot banger also kept out the crows, pigeons and occasional seagull that spied through the windows and sensed there was no food to be had amid the racket. Mr. Ketchum reinforced the idea of there being no food by shouting in bird language whenever he walked around the bird house. If he saw a warbler relaxing on the verandah post, he would scream toward it in vowels all pronounced glub-glub, that there were no seeds or worms in the parlour.

Chapter 3

Napanee Employed

The manager used the employee's lounge for mid-week pep talks to staff. The three dozen donuts were never enough to fill the appetites of all attendees. Attendance was compulsory, although enthusiasm was not. At one meeting, an employee fell asleep sitting up in an uncomfortable bridge chair. He snored until Napanee poked him in the shoulder with a ballpoint pen. Applause rose around the lounge.

"You are the best boss. You're a real dream," Napanee said.

"Why are you lathering me up, Nap?"

"I mean it. You listen to employees. You protect us from drunk customers like you did last week. That guy followed me around the store until you gave him a one-two."

"Yeah, he was drunk. I just gave him a slice to the windpipe. He smelt mean, that f..."

The store manager swore in several different ways. When he spoke to people he respected, like Napanee, he would use the F-word playfully, as if chastising himself for doing so, as if imitating others who had an uncontrollable mouth. When he was in conversation with peers or subordinates, he tried to adjective as many objects and people with swear words without fear of repetition or staccato. Anatomical parts, various positions of coitus and evacuation of feces filled his sentences, giving his speech a rich double context. It forced the listener to detect whether he was angry. It was never clear whether he was truly talking about stocking the shelves or what he saw through the neighbor's window in the middle of the night. That was where his leadership quality lay. His diction smelled of the street fighter and the curious bystander. He evoked attention while he spoke, so much so that no-one ever dared interrupt. His written memos to staff could have been written for a church bulletin board; his verbal explanation of them was another matter.

It was so simple being a store manager. There was nothing to do but react to subordinates' deficiencies. His own supervisor had told him not to call unless he had good things to say. The supervisor trusted his loyalty, which was the only thing that counted. He guessed that loyalty existed because of a quirk reported to him from different sources.

The manager would leave the store every two hours for no apparent reason, and always in a rush. Sometimes, he had one arm in his coat sleeve as he walked through the automatic doors. He was never gone on these occasions for longer than ten minutes. When this activity first came to light, the supervisor suspected smoking was the cause. As it persisted, the suspicion turned to drug encounters, even an illicit affair. The assistant floor manager was asked to follow the manager on his get-aways; and the report came back that he kept frequenting the donut shop at the end of the parking lot.

"Why don't you get your donuts and coffee before you come to work?"

The manager did not understand what the supervisor was saying. His face struggled to reply.

"Why are you always at the donut place?"

"To pee."

"What's wrong with the store facilities."

"I can't pee in the store…It's my store."

"Your store has an employees' bathroom. What's wrong with it?"

"Nothing wrong with it…I just don't want to desecrate it, so I go to the shop. It doesn't feel right working in a place, earning a living, and peeing there too."

Price lived in a book bin. One parent did not know he existed. The other wanted only the best for him at the right price. That is why his living quarters bothered neither. Price's friends were passers-by, his close friends were the books piled up around him. The bin was a carpeted bathtub, covered in beige shag after being donated by the founder's family. Mortimer Ketchum's will specifically conditioned the monetary bequest for the Library with an injunction that the bathtub he loved so much be *placed within it for all to appreciate*". There was much to appreciate in the 1910's porcelain tub. It had lion's paws for legs, prominent claws and ankle bones fashioned from brass. The drain had the lips of a gargoyle. Anyone with a brief imagination could picture a boyish Mortimer lost in a pool of suds, worried that his feet would be swallowed by the devil during a bath. A larger man would have no problem fitting his back into the contours of the tub and resting his arms over the generously wide rim.

No-one ever revealed why he loved the tub, if that is what he did. Maybe he hated it, or maybe it reminded him of his mother or the nannies who bathed him. Perhaps he had no emotional connection to it, positive or negative. His stipulation could have been a way of reminding the public of his presence, more than his bust at the entrance or his name branding the building could.

Whatever the reason for its presence, the head librarian found a way to deal with it. His cousin, a carpet layer, coated it inside and out with adhesive then applied the entirety of the shag remnant that had lain in a roll in his shop for years. It was vacuumed from time to time, but otherwise needed no maintenance as a return book bin. Children always crawled in and out of it under the pretense of retrieving a book. Some could not get in; some could not get out; and some fell asleep hypnotized by the ceiling fan blades.

The bathtub was more than a cradle. It was Mr. Ketchum's mortmain, his dead inflated hand, newly carpeted, hiding the lines between his fingers. It was his teacup, his soup bowl, any receptacle he had used and breathed into during his moments of rest or enjoyment of a simple luxury. A child caught in his cradling hand had nothing to fear, nothing to complain about and nothing to leave for.

An expressive woman wearing what looked like a shower cap on her head would come every second day, just to sit by the bin facing the infant with an over-sized children's book in her hands. First she would wave the closed book, creating a draft that lifted the curls on his head. Once that delightful sensation drew a wide smile across his face, she opened the covers and quickly snapped them closed, creating a clap and a wind. He brought his hands together under his chin. After she would leave, Price would stare at the book lying at his feet, pressing it from time to time with his index finger. The book was a wind machine; it had a voice, and many more invisible facets.

Once, two boys stood near the shelves tossing spitballs and flicking pencils toward the bin. As one of them was about to toss a handful of staples his way, a volume dislodged from the top shelf, opened like a parachute and struck the boy in the face. Another followed, hitting his friend on the shoulder with the end of its spine. It was easy to see, even for a baby, that books protected, talked, and kept company.

Napanee brought her constant friend Cheryl to meet the manager, just to show him off. When her friend mentioned she had been to Woodstock but had been too stoned to remember how she had gotten pregnant, the manager insisted they all go out for lunch at the Mexican restaurant in the strip mall across the street. The food he ordered was too hot. Cheryl, whom he had been calling Honey, put an end to his droopy-eyelid look by saying she had three children and was married to an actuary.

To Cheryl, Napanee was a hero, raising her son on her own, teaching him to be independent. Cheryl needed so much help at home, she wondered how Napanee had done it. Of course, Cheryl had the full support and company of her parents. Still, Napanee had the strength she did not have. She wanted to be like her as far as she could to gain an insight into that strength.

Cheryl told her husband they would not have sex until Napanee did, as a show of empathy.

"No one I know wants to touch as much as you do. You like to cling, don't you. Keep away from me unless you ask first," she asserted.

"This is not normal," her husband would say.

"You're not normal. And don't touch or smell my clothes. It gives me the creeps."

"You've become frigid," he said in despair.

"No, I've become free. If you want something, make an appointment."

The ancient Sabine women had a community cause: Cheryl's was good enough for her, although strangely she did not make Napanee aware of it. When Napanee would find another mate, Cheryl would then engage in empathetic intimacy to show her it did not matter unless Napanee thought it mattered. The evening following a major marital argument, Cheryl dyed her hair blond, shouting in histrionic rhetoric to her spouse, Go home to your parents.

Napanee and Cheryl were comrades-in-arms, especially because they shared the experience, the once-in-a-lifetime personal revolution that profoundly changed perceptions and attitudes. Unlike the after-shocks of the Industrial Revolution, which may have dictated how consumers in the late 1900s related to their products, the birth of the automated teller machine, opened and developed their imagination on a metaphysical level.

"Napanee, you don't have to count the cash. The machine is always right."

"Until it's wrong. I got ten bucks more than I punched in, and you know, there was no way to give it back."

"And no-one licks their fingers counting the bills. No more lines or stupid girls at the bank."

Their spirit, chained by the problem of cash flow when they ventured out each day, was liberated by the omnipresence of the ATM. Once freed from the concerns of carrying cash, they had more time to reassess what progress they had made in life, and who most needed their attention.

Napanee's father Gerald followed his own plan with little deviation, looking first in the obvious, then in the tangential and finally in the obscure places. On the other hand, Harry's parents, who lived in the mid-west, had heard from their son twice since his flight from matrimony, although could not give his location. Not that they were being protective: they had not even known he had abandoned Napanee, nor that she was pregnant, nor that she had given birth. The last and only time they had seen her was at the wedding.

"Harry told us he was on the road, finding money for the deal of a lifetime. He said he was working on it with Barry," his mother said, nodding to her husband Sam.

"Who is Barry?" Gerald asked, reminding her to speak directly into the phone.

"Who is Barry? Barry is his other self. A childhood friend he loves like a brother. They were always inseparable. He was an usher, not the best man, remember? They used to call them Harry and Barry. Remember, at the wedding they sang a silly song, Harry-Barry?" Harry's mother reminisced without any end in sight.

"So where can I find Barry?" Gerald suspected he would never find an answer.

"We can't help you there."

"Where does he live? What does he do? Where was he last?" Gerald exhausted most of his questions, thankful that the in-laws did not live in the same city.

"Oh, I don't know. We actually never met him," she said regretfully. "Sam, did we ever meet Barry? Sam says no, but he's Harry's closest friend."

"He was at the wedding, you said. He must be on the wedding list."

Memories of the wedding were as obscure as the where-abouts of the invitation list. She remembered more about pre-paring for the event than being there. Maybe it was because very few guests at the wedding knew each other. Harry did not have many friends, or at least friends who cared enough to show up at a wedding. Napanee knew a lot of people from different circles, kitchen ware parties, bargain events, fairs and markets and meet-a-mate weekends, none of which overlapped. Doing the arrangements at the tables posed no problem. Guests were seated alphabetically.

"Do you have his address?" Gerald asked impatiently.

"No... No. Harry delivered the invitations by hand to his own friends. I didn't actually see Barry at the wedding. Did you, Sam? Sam says there were too many people. He doesn't remember any of them... Who does the baby look like?"

"Don't know. Haven't seen it yet," Gerald said almost inaudibly. He had lost his impulse to cross-examine any further.

"When can we see it? This would be our fifth grandchild. They all have so many different names; I can't remember most of them. What's his name?"

"I haven't spoken to it by name."

Harry was attracted to Napanee's way of acting rich. While her family lived modestly, he suspected hidden trust funds. They met while he was earning money walking neighborhood dogs between deals. He married the whole family, which preferred that he leave his town and set up the matrimonial home nearby. Actually, in her parents' house.

The wedding had been spectacular, judging from the photographs. The band leader insisted on a bonus each overtime half-hour they played. Harry directed him to his father-in-law. Gerald ran out of cash at one in the morning. Looking amid the four hundred guests who had stayed till that hour, he found three he could borrow from without too much embarrassment. Napanee's mother had drunk too much to be helpful to the party organizer. At one point, she cried into her mousse dessert because some of the invitees had not come. She had sent invitations to Queen Elizabeth, who did not respond; to three heads of state, whose secretaries mailed regrets; and to a baseball pitcher who sent back the invitation with his autograph. They would have made a solid good table, she thought, to the left of the head table. She loved the Queen as a female role model and friend of horses.

"Any idea of the business you want to get into?" Gerald had asked. He did respect his wife's intuition that Harry was ideal for his daughter.

"Opportunity is what I'm looking for, Dad," Harry said with something called glee.

"Don't call me Dad. It makes me nervous."

Napanee had let Harry worry about seduction, while she fretted about matching her shoes to her handbag and to her hat. She only half-heard what he said about she being a goddess, the one for him, his first really great love, his difficulty in mastering French while briefly at a Swiss boarding school. She plainly was not interested in having him suck her cheek all night if it meant being distracted.

The engagement was quick, the wedding quick. She told him to do what he had to after the wedding. The deal was that if he didn't talk, he would get his pleasure. The other part of the deal was that she liked the light on because she might want to arrange her coupons.

"I can't work with the light on," Harry complained.

"I'm lying here like a bag of flour. Take as much flour as you want. Put on a blindfold if you have to. What else do you want from me?"

During the six months the marriage lasted, Harry suffocated under the sense of togetherness. Gerald planned the vacation for all four in the Florida Keys. Her mother took the couple with her to bingo night every few weeks, which she loved because it was so democratic. Her parents gave him a dog they pre-named Bull. Harry frequently looked into the mirror to admire the sleekness of his black hair and the sharpness of the part in the middle of his head. Bull, a very possessive animal, took to jumping into Harry's way during his admiration sessions at the mirror in the washroom. Gerald then renamed the dog Eisenhower, and reminded Harry not to call him Bull. He then changed the name again to McArthur.

Every few evenings, her father would quiz him.

"Did you find the opportunity, Harry?"

"Didn't go out today. I took the dog to the vet. Worms."

Four months after the wedding, Harry began taking week-end and then week-long business trips financed by her parents. They knew what destinations he was visiting from his tickets and credit card receipts but had little idea what he was doing. Gerald had immediate suspicions and was geared for a confrontation. He did not want to lose Harry because he kept Napanee occupied. Better put, he did not want to lose him for any reason other than Harry's own fault. Gerald was never warm to him since he did not deserve warmth. Whenever Harry talked sense, sincere sense, he was prepared to listen. His sensitivity to Harry's sincerity was acute, even if there were only trace samplings of it. Harry's problem was that he usually sounded eager and extractive, something his voice and demeanor poorly masked.

"Real estate, if you want to know. Real estate management of time-shares, Dad. An entirely new concept."

"Sounds great. Do you need investment money?" Gerald asked.

"Yes... I can look for bank financing, although... family money would be easier."

"It's a waste of money to pay interest, but it's probably a good chunk for a starter deal," Gerald suggested.

"Four hundred thousand for entry. Not a lot to spend on your daughter's future. Her independence..."

"We can work it out."

"When? The deal closes next week. I had to work my way in."

Once he got the money, Harry concluded he had been blinded by Napanee's beauty. She had no soul. She did not understand him. She spent most of the day looking at catalogues or shopping. She was really not his kind of girl. Shawna on the weekends was. The last thing Napanee had told Harry before he left for good was that she was having trouble with her period. Not seizing the significance, he impatiently told her to fix it.

Chapter 4

Gerald And Harry Rumble

Napanee's father had nothing in common with Harry except that neither man could sit still for more than a few seconds. Harry was not intellectually driven: his stand-up, sit-down gyrations were more motivated by smells in the air or an imperceptible noise than philosophic curiosity. Her father was motivated by genuine curiosity and the boredom of its non-fulfillment.

When they first met, Gerald made the mistake of asking Harry if he had read any good books lately. Harry said his mother would not let him read books because he tended to tear strips off the pages to chew. This was a habit he had developed when he started attending high school. He had chewed his way through Algebra, then Red Badge of Courage and World History. When he developed a form of cankers in the right side of his mouth, the doctor told his mother to leave gum all around the house. Harry left so many gum wads in clumsy places, his mother gave him a telephone book. His tongue was black within days.

"Want to know what's wrong with books, Dad? They're too predictable. I could start reading a novel and by page 5, I could tell you how it ends. So what's the point? They're all the same."

"I don't know what you're talking about. They're not all the same. Although I don't like novels. I prefer history and biography and business."

"All the same. You know what's good? Horoscopes, poems in birthday cards. They should put that poetry in books. Everyone reads them."

Gerald's middle name was Harold, which he denied having. Gerald thought Harry was a park pigeon, while Harry thought of his father-in-law when he stared at him, as a grazing rhinoceros, swaying his head lethargically back and forth as the flies buzzed his eyelids. Harry exuded want: he was little more than a neck with an open hand for a face. Gerald hated waiting for Harry to ask for something. Once asked, he was rid of his company.

They were both thin, had stubble, blue eyes, hated golf, and enjoyed the same beer. Their parents came from the same city. They needed buffers between them when they found themselves in the same room. There was nothing to talk about that would last a minute. Each other was what they hated in themselves.

Gerald was not the best father-in-law. He never had the chance to be one, to get close to Harry. Although he experienced as much attraction as repulsion with him, Gerald was now bent on getting unbearably close to him.

Why was Harry the way he was? His father had never beat him. His mother had never abandoned him. In fact, his parents had never demanded anything of him except to lock the front door or the back door whenever he left. Even that he did not do well. His problem was shutting the doors, applying the extra energy to pull the lock into a clicked position so that no-one would have to finish off what he had started. For the same reason, he could not be bothered to pull away the banana peel to get to the last third of its meat, or to gather his shoe laces into a bow instead of dragging them underfoot. He loved his own hair, although not enough to replace the cap on the shampoo bottle or to pull the strands of it out of his many brushes.

"I'll find him in a Soho fashion boutique or a Key West lime pie. Wherever he's hiding, I'll make sure he pays for what he did to my daughter," Gerald said to his wife as he gardened.

By profession, Gerald worked as an aircraft engineer with attention to the impact of detail. As an investor, he had learned the theory of risk probability and random walk. Where could Harry be? The only way to find out was to superimpose an element of randomness over Harry's predictable patterns.

According to his airline flight books, he had gone to three cities ten times in three months. According to his car rental trips, Harry kept to a two hundred mile radius of the city and convenience hotels. According to his meal tabs, he preferred steak houses and sweet shops. Gerald could have retraced those haunts or sent someone to do it. Or he could have called Harry's dentist in town to see when his next visit was booked.

Harry loved his own teeth, which he often tried to mirror in the blade of his butter knife during a family meal. Flossing in public never bothered Harry, although he made a useless attempt to be discreet. The credit card statement showed two recent visits to the dentist, who was Gerald's classmate.

"I see you're making a living off of Harry's mouth. I'm paying the bill, you know."

"The boy cracked a tooth on a gumball," the dentist said, sucking on the sterilized canine tooth of one of last year's patients.

He found it gave him a greater appreciation of the shape of canines, which he personally preferred over molars. Most of the molars he had seen in his professional career had been drilled, filled, cracked or removed. Canines, on the other hand, kept their shape and strength even though they might have lost their colour. He could not imagine a world without teeth, which is why he often said insects do not have dental problems.

"Has he finished his treatment?"

"One more visit to put in the final crown. Tomorrow at 2 p.m."

Gerald waited outside the dental office building with a former machinist who brought a pair of pliers with him. When Harry cleared the outside door, Gerald beckoned his surprised son-in-law. Catching him off guard, the machinist pushed Harry into the back of their waiting van. The machinist was sitting on Harry's shoulder blades, rummaging through his teeth, until he found what he thought was a newly installed crown. Applying industrial force to the handles of his pliers, he was able to crack the crown, leaving Harry to spit out the shards.

From the front seat, but not bothering to turn around, Gerald said: "Now that you're comfortable, I want you to sign this consent to divorce, and custody and alimony. And I also want my four hundred thousand dollars back. Will you give it back to me or does my friend have to give you a manicure?"

His son-in-law was dutiful, signing all the documents, calling the bank and ultimately wishing his friends his best as they left him in a field.

Standing corn obscured his view of the road. He walked the wrong way until he found himself on the edge of a pasture. Not far from him, a tree surrounded by seven dairy cows gave a wide circle of shade. A block of salt stuck out of the mud and manure. When the first cow saw Harry, it coughed and barked like an oversized dog, baring its gums to him and then to its social group. The others did the same, some grinding their teeth, splashing the mud and kicking the salt. Harry definitely heard not moo-ing; moo-ing was a peaceful sound. These cows were angry, maybe vicious. He ran back into the cornfield toward the rumble of a truck.

Harry could not understand Gerald's need for revenge. Life has its rough edges, people have to adjust, the world turns, there is no room for punishment. Being punitive brings back memories but provides no solutions. Of course, Harry did not have the opportunity to speak sanely with Gerald, whom he considered to be insane.

Reaching the road from the field, Harry saw a cyclist wearing a Superman outfit, red cape flowing perfectly above the rear wheel, smiling, apparently not on any mission of urgency. The cape fluttered not like a flag, but like the supple tail feathers of a tropical bird. Harry breathed deeply, wondering why he needed a bicycle.

Gerald did not take pleasure in revenge. He was duty-bound to rectify a wrong. Harry was not capable of introspection, guilt or self-reform: it was therefore Gerald's duty to teach him a lesson. The intensity of his drive was not as searing as the honor killings and mutilations he had studied in the practices of Hamurabi, and all his modern legal and cultural counterparts. In most places, there were no equivalents to the Biblical Cities of Refuge where the manslaughterer could find sanctuary from the avenging family of the victim.

The innate notion that spilt blood cried out for remedy need not have been confined to any particular expression. Gerald did not want to kill because that would be counter-productive. Harry could not be let loose in the same society without knowing he had done something fundamentally wrong and had victimized the innocent.

Chapter 5

Motherhood Begins

It came easily to her. Of the fourteen thousand items on sale, Napanee knew the prices of thirteen thousand five hundred. In the lunch room, one floor clerk would greet her in the morning.

"So how much do the shower curtain hooks, twelve in a package, cost?"

The cashiers preferred to consult her rather than the assistant manager they called Toll-free, if the tag on an item was missing or suspiciously altered. For twelve consecutive months, she remained star employee. Toll-free liked to tuck her pay cheque into her back pocket. More recently, he would insert company pens and sticker pads into the breast pocket of her blouse. At the end of each month, he lovingly conducted the star employee ceremony, pinning the medallion on her blouse far below her collar.

"Now you look like a star, Napanee."

"You like the pinning thing."

"I want our employees to feel empowered. Anything I can do?"

"You're the boss. You give me things to do, until I say buzz off."

Saturday nights, Toll-free wore a top hat; a Fred Astaire pop-up, glinting black hat that drew attention away from his tee-shirt or sweats or whatever informal wear he had on. Haircut days meant the hat would slip lower on his head, bending his fleshy ear-tops outward, as if they were supporting the brim. His grandfather wore a top hat on Sundays to grace the day. Toll-free wore the same hat on party nights to grace the party. After a while at the bar, patrons grew used to his image, not that of a squat Abraham Lincoln, but of a cheesy local politician in the 1920s. It did though dignify his face, as it dignified a hat-rack or a staircase post. It elevated any pro-fane body to a formal stature, something shoes, a tie or a vest could never alone do. The hat was magnetic, as awesome in its symmetry as the oval of an ordinary egg. At the store, Toll-free was not magnetic.

During the Blue Monday Sale, he placed something in Napanee's back pocket. Napanee found nothing there except Toll-free's unwanted attention. It happened twice during the day.

"You're touching me a lot," she said as a matter of fact.

"I don't hear any complaints."

"Who would I complain to if I wanted to?" she asked for the record.

"The Manager. But he's dying to do the same thing." Toll-free thought it a masterly way of endearing himself to her.

They were standing in the bathroom accessories aisle. Looking both ways to confirm no shoppers were in the area, Napanee asked him coyly to adjust the pin on her chest. As he reached out to realize his dreams, she slapped over-sized Blue Monday stickers over his eyes and forehead, temporarily blinding him. Then she clicked on the loud-speakers at the end of the aisle and announced a price reduction on bath mats for the next ten minutes.

When Toll-free was pulling off the stickers, he could not avoid ripping out some of the hair from his eyebrows and eyelashes. He also knocked over boxes of towel racks and soap dishes while flailing his arms. He did not feel defeated or foolish. His pain was righteous. He had a right to snoop around females the same way a dog put its nose in garbage to feed itself. He wanted to curse her, yet that would have intensified his pain. In order to calm himself, he simply recalled how close he got to touching Napanee's treasure.

Toll-free felt like a beaten anvil when he went to the barber shop to re-arrange his appearance. With twelve hyperactive barbers on duty on a first-come, first-served basis, one took him as soon as he entered. Clearing the vestiges of the previous cut from his chair with a sweep of the back of the hand, he invited him with the palm of the same hand to have a seat. At first, he looked at the mess on Toll-free's forehead, then at his fellow barber.

"You stole my towel", he sniped.

"Did not", his neighbor pouted with his back to him.

"You wiped your hands on it."

"Okay, 'cause I had to", his neighbor conceded.

"Listen to him: he had to!" the barber said in minor disgust as he dug his scissors into a clump of Toll-free's hair. He told his customer that if he wanted to rip out his eyebrows, there was a better way to do it. Everyone agreed Toll-free needed a professional guiding hand and new look.

Her father's suggestion was to talk to the family lawyer. Days later, she was advised to accept a two hundred thousand dollar settlement offer from the store management and a hush-up agreement, which she did. That was when the store manager was promoted out to head office. The settlement confirmed Gerald's trust in the lawyer which was originally based on his face which looked like a beaten old pot. The texture of his long hands was soft steel-wool, comforting, with the potential for abrasion. On weekends, he served as a blacksmith at an equestrian school, banging bits of iron into irregularly shaped nails he sold for pennies each to the neighbours.

Napanee was filled with a spirit of self economic worth. She had not known intangibles like dignity and privacy, things that could not be properly pictured or sold in a catalogue, had a market price and could be sullied and restored to the owner for subsequent and repeated re-sullying. She wondered with her mother what other treasure she had hidden intangibly or otherwise somewhere in her legal psyche. To learn that an insult could be cashed in for so much money meant that a broken fingernail, a scratch on her arm, a sprained ankle were worth all the more. Her entire essence, once weighed in all its attributes and parts, was easily a billionaire's delight. Being so expensive gave her every reason to think and act like a monarch or a fortress of gold.

Many would have said the baby Price was precocious simply because of his diction. At age fifteen months, he was chubby, bubbly. Living in the Library so long had brought him into contact with thousands of well-wishers who passed the book bin at the strictly prescribed times, making faces, waving at both him and the student guard who watched him closely after three attempted snatchings. The baby had been stimulated by so many greetings, so many different beings, all leaving the same impression: the natural state of a person is happiness provided all the rules are respected. One of these rules was standing in line nicely for a turn to see. As one person disappeared, another popped up with a fresh face. Young children asked the simple questions:

"Is he real?"

"Is he alive?"

"What does he eat?"

"Where is his home?"

"Did someone leave him here?"

Strangers taught Price something very concrete, a personal skill he would later use to great advantage. When children and mothers crowded around the tub, they invariably displayed a joyous hand, a palm with five widespread wiggling fingers to hold his attention. The open hand, fingers mimicking a stick drawing of the sun's rays, to him became a universal greeting of friendship, a signal by the one approaching that only happiness was intended.

To add to his allure, he smelled like a baby should. His skin was smooth and slightly perfumed with baby breath. His diapers were constantly changed so that he would never develop a rash or feel the discomfort of irritation. His sleepers were usually new, which meant his little fingers could sense the velvet finish on the surface of his belly. Dribble did not have a chance to dry on his cheek or under the folds of his chins. His attendants were quick to dry him, tamp his face, fuss all over, give him the treatment of an exotic and hardy flower. Many agreed he looked wise, maybe because of his grooming, maybe for his lack of unjustified crankiness.

The first thing he said was not a word but a complete sentence. As he sat throwing baby books over the guardrail, he could be heard saying a babyish "Have a nice day" to new and old members. The truth is that there were too many new members to handle. When the factory outlets grew up near the Library, shoppers came to relax in the quiet reading rooms and surreptitiously eat lunch. That crowd had been neatly shamed into becoming members by the head librarian. Price now brought a new class of members: the curious baby lovers who were incidental shoppers and knew the hours.

Napanee knew something was missing. All around the Library, mothers sat on the floor reading to their smallest children. It left a desire so strong she went by Price's bin at the slow time before the lunch rush. She read a few lines from the store sales brochures, emphasizing with wide eyes: "Hurry while supplies last!" That brought on an applauding face. Price clapped his hands clumsily. Another day saw her back at the bin reading from a product description: "Limited to parts and labour!" she whoopied. Price was overjoyed, waving his arms in a jumping-jacks routine. It was a thrill to see him react to something she had stimulated. The feeling of this thrill was novel. She was moved to say, "Be honest, Price. And people will respect your warranty."

Napanee was changing. It started when she misquoted the price of a box of moth balls. The next day, she arrived minutes late for work. At closing hour, she had a desire to take the baby home with her for the first time. She cried out over the circulation desk: "Price, my baby, come to me. We're leaving the book bin for good."

She hugged him as she would a fashion designer. As far as Price could understand, this was another fleeting reader. But she had more to say, with a wisdom only a mother could have. As she slowly pirouetted near the bin, pointing to the distant mountains of books and nearer valleys of aisles, Napanee confided in him.

"Be true to yourself. Being true means looking good, and being wise enough to spot a bargain. I'm taking you home now, to a new home. It's different because there are no best sellers, but otherwise it's the same."

The baby's yawn consumed its whole face. When his face was recomposed, his cheeks shone scarlet, very much like the disproportioned cheeks of an infant in a Renaissance religious painting. Those babies were often depicted as chubby miniature men held by the oddly angled hands of the mother. Price was holy, as were his surroundings, because he had survived, and all around him, life was being nurtured. Price closed his eyes slowly, taking in the awesome vision of the dangling strands of her blond hair. He wondered in an infantile way how it was she was here after closing time and what was happening to his bin.

Napanee enrolled him in a day-care centre where they taught all the toddlers their most important word - *"Mine"*. That word, once learned, ensured belongings did not get lost, and did not travel to two-year old thieves. His caregiver said Price spent a lot of time stacking the books, smoothing out the sand and picking up litter.

On the way home, whenever she had the occasion to pick him up at day care, she told him: "Because you have no-one to be your father, not that you need anyone, I will take you to the ball game. We will stop at the off-arena parking at the last minute and walk through the crowds of scalpers. We'll play one off against another as the time for the game gets closer. We'll buy hundred dollar tickets and then, before going into the stadium, we'll sell them for two hundred bucks. People will trust a female scalper more than a man. Especially one holding a little guy like you. See, Price, there is a game inside, and a game outside. It doesn't matter if we never get inside because we still see a game. And we're in it. So don't worry about the father and son thing. We'll handle it better than anyone else."

Even as he grew past infancy, Price took great joy in strangers. There were new faces, new insights, quick transitions. Everyone thought it unusual how he immediately took to people he had never met. Whenever Napanee had the time to look in on him at school or the playground with his nanny, she immediately could detect through mother's radar if anything troubled him. That is why Napanee was so accomplished.

She also knew enough to consult experienced mothers, like her friend. Cheryl prohibited her husband's parents from seeing their two children. Napanee was curious. Cheryl did not like the idea of other people rummaging through her daughter and son as if they were going through the odds-and-ends on her night table. The base of the lamp on her night table had a hairline crack. It was all private; her children were private to her.

"What do those people want. Why don't they sit in a rocking chair and look at my kids' pictures. They don't even send presents. My husband has to remind them when their birthdays are. They say they're the ones who remind him. Can you believe it?"

Napanee told her a mother's instinct is like gravity. Whatever a mother feels is best for the children is best. In-laws, grandparents are just invited guests. Napanee approved because private things are private. In intervals of weakness, Cheryl's in-laws did see them, although always for brief visits in her presence, and always at her home. She did not let the children eat grandma's home-baked cookies or listen to grand-dad read a story. She would tell them their presence scared the children. Napanee suggested she not let them baby-sit or to take the children on outings or pick them up from school. Cheryl did not want her children to mix with their cousins on her husband's side. When he asked why they were not going *en famille* to his nephew's birthday party, she said the birthday boy had a germy face. Cheryl kept no pictures of her in-laws in the home. Whenever they would call by telephone, she said the children were asleep or watching television.

"The important thing is to be consistent. I'm sure your in-laws love you and respect you for it," Napanee concluded.

Gerald never had a son. He did not miss one. The idea of having a grandson made no immediate impact on him, except to make him wonder what he would be called. Grandpa worked, since he always saw himself as the encompassing patrician of the family without the expected acknowledgment or overt gratitude.

As Price grew, Gerald began to see direct points of connection, so that the boy, little by little, was not simply Napanee's son. He was also Gerald's grandson or someone who was part of him. Only due to that awareness of connection did Gerald first tell Price the story of when he was in an airplane flying over a lot of trees. The narrative came to no conclusion. It had many sound effects: flapping lips created the motor, while flapping arms created the illusion of dangerous flying. The story suffered slight development by repetition over the years. By the time Price was six, Gerald in the airplane was beginning to sound thin.

"What's the end of the story?" Price asked one night before sleep.

So Gerald began the long process over the next few years of filling in the details.

"I was a soldier in the airplane. I was a navigator and told the pilot where to go because we didn't want to crash."

Aside from those details, which fascinated Price, the story went no further over the next few months except to explain what his uniform looked like.

The major issue, when Price was seven years old, was that he had forgotten how to pee. Never before a bed wetter, he suddenly encountered difficulty in his regularity. Cheryl could not figure out what the root cause was, so she reassured Napanee the way to deal with it was to simply attack it. The problem started at the same time Price got frustrated doing a crossword puzzle in the newspaper. He did not have the knowledge of celebrities' names to complete the top and bottom acrosses. He wanted the words he knew to fit: fitting them into the structure brought him a level of pleasurable completeness.

"He thinks he did something wrong and now he's punishing himself."

"Cheryl, that's psychiatry.'

"Maybe he wants to fix the world by drawing attention to himself."

"You mean maybe he wants to fix me. Is there something about me he doesn't like?"

"Can't imagine. He owes you everything."

She recommended pouring warm water over Price's fingers at rhythmic intervals. It did not work. Try to run the tap water while he slept. It did not help. Run a humidifier that made a whooshing sound in his room. No effect. Take him to the zoo to see animals peeing and telling him the whole world does it. No change. Give him a large glass of warm chocolate milk every hour. Uncertain, because Price smelled the steam and licked the froth without taking much of a gulp. No, one Sunday, after standing in the rain for an hour collecting water in a cup, he told his mother who had just returned from an auction, he remembered how to do it.

Cheryl saw Price was testing nature to see whether it was good to be irregular.

"I think he decided that the way things are is the way they should be".

"You see, Cheryl, I would never have the insight on this that you have."

Once Price was straightened out, Gerald bought him a bicycle sporting streamers hanging from the handlebars. Gerald taught him how to ride on the back lawn, although he would have to admit that his grandson had no fear in pushing himself to balance. Once Price saw that speed was the key to balance and that the forces of nature could be triggered by an active push-off, he insisted Gerald let go of the seat to permit him to ride on his own.

Shortly after that accomplishment, Price told his grandfather:

"It's like being in an airplane, probably... You know that story you always tell me about you up in the sky. Nothing happens. You're just in an airplane."

"It was during the war. We flew over a little city, and we didn't do anything. But I'll tell you later what we did when we flew over the trees."

"It's a no-good story. Nothing happens."

Chapter 6

Gerald Loves Price

Gerald loved the smell of new shoes, gasoline and window putty. which he tried to pass on to Price. Price loved the smell of Gerald's coffee table books as they opened. The combination of binder's glue, paper acid and ink was as pungently attractive as the scent of an orchid. A book is a mechanical device: pages on a hinge, sequential and encrypted. Those with stitched binding could stay open at any page. Others could easily suffer a cracked spine if one pressed down on their open center. Books are like fruit in various story flavours, each with its own personality, each copy newer than the first.

"Have you notice Price that the pages make no noise when you flip them?"

"They make a wind."

"No. Each book makes its own sound. That's the voice. Older ones have a little paper smell, like old newspapers. That's the odour. Forget about what's on the cover. They all have a personality in the way they feel and act… Know what I hate? When people write in a book or underline."

"Mommy does that in her magazines."

"Magazines smell like plastic. They're totally different."

The miniature dictionaries and trade editions of hard-covers fit into the inner pocket of Price's windbreaker, largely unnoticed. Had the book format not been invented in the Renaissance period or before, the stores and libraries would now be filled with scrolls or feuilletons or magazine-type literature. Imagine reading a scientific work in newspaper format. Scrolls always require thicker paper to avoid tearing and cracking. If they had wooden rollers, Price's windbreaker could never have accommodated their weight and bulk. His pocket held his only treasure.

That is why he volunteered at the school library after hours putting away books on the shelves. It earned him high praise from the librarian who had seen him re-shelving during book hour while the other children were oblivious to the disorder. That is why he pushed an older pupil over in his chair, making him break his backward fall with the back of his head. The victim lay still, his body still seated in the chair, horizontal to the floor. The librarian thought he was unconscious until he jumped to his feet, ready to fight. The small ribbon of blood from his nose made a curious arch around the edge of his lips. He tried not to look bewildered or dizzy. Whatever he was trying to say was not coming out right.

A teacher intervened, separating the belligerents with her body.

"Why did you do that Price?"

"He tore a page out of the encyclopedia."

"By accident?"

"No, it was like he was tearing a little bird apart."

The principal called in Gerald because he could not locate Napanee. He told the boy violence was not the way to settle a problem, that damaging a book did not call for injuring a fellow student and that it was not his business anyway. The principal was not getting through.

"Do you hear what I'm saying?"

"You don't understand books."

Price pouted, his lower lip emphasizing he would do it again. He was sent home for a few days during which he managed to finish most of the crossword games in a book Cheryl had given him.

Gerald liked to think he had raised his grandson, at least between the uneven attention his wife and Napanee paid him. Over the years, they moved him through a number of schools, each time bargaining a better deal on tuition. For the same reason, there were multiple piano teachers.

Gerald taught him the unhurried stability of digging up tree roots, stripping away weeds, using soil conditioners and pruning rose bushes. He also fostered the deep love Price began to feel for Gerald's dog. The day Gerald put the dog down, he told Price it had run away and was probably killed on the highway. When Price told him it was a fable, Gerald retrieved the dog's body from the vet and told him to see for himself.

He had convinced the boy by bringing an omen. What a pathetic way to earn respect from a descendant, he thought. Yet the act of bringing omens to convince disbelievers had ancient roots among the religious and the pagan. Bringing the dead for revival occurs in the Bible; not, of course, a dead dog. It was a testimony, an act of contrition and pleading. Gerald did what he could, but there was something wrong.

"Price, I wish you would believe me when I tell you things."

"You don't believe yourself."

"Alright. I didn't want you to be upset with what I had to do to the dog. It was suffering."

"Animals don't just run away to die. They know the rules like we know the rules."

"It trusted me to the end. It saw the end was coming."

Twelve days after his twelfth birthday, at noon, Price punched a woman in the nose, something he did not later regret. The woman was a driver who had run a red light, just in time to hit the side of another car in the intersection. The other driver emerged from his car, his nose and elbow bloodied.

Price had been standing at the light about to cross on the green. He had seen the collision, watched the woman run from her car to take care of the injured driver. She repeated it was an accident; she had not noticed the red light. As she shouted in the intersection for an ambulance, Price walked up to her and punched her.

"You're supposed to respect the lights. You had no right to have an accident. You should not be driving if you make accidents," he said as she sat slightly off the road where Price had sent her reeling.

She tamped her cut lip with her sleeve, muttering, "Are you crazy or something. Who do you think you are? Are you the police? It's none of your business."

Disobedience of a basic traffic rule struck him as being so fundamentally illogical and wrong, he had to express himself. What he witnessed was an unraveling of a social pattern, the onset of a chaos so outrageous as to challenge his comfort in the harmony of street order. He stayed to tell the police how disturbed the incident had made him. He was arrested as soon as the officer could make out what had happened.

Price was so friendly with all the police staff, they doubted his normalcy. The badges, encrusted with laurel crests and numbered, were encrypted with authority. Authority spoke cleanly, truthfully, and never had to repeat itself. The officer taking down the incident report did not relate to him coldly: he asked officially, and noted the responses clinically. The whole exercise was refreshing because it was basic and structural. Price sat upright, his answers prefaced with "Sir". Nothing was hidden nor worth hiding.

"You know what you did was wrong," the officer said in the name of the law.

"I know I had to do it. If it was wrong, I will not do it again."

The easiest way to strengthen their relationship after settling with the assault victim and the police was to take Price on a long trip. Gerald was no longer worried about being rebuffed by Price because he was not his father. Price never used the word 'father': he had no need to, nor any occasion. Gerald took his responsibilities in hand, which meant making sure his grandson was fed, clothed and able to spiritually develop. His secular spirituality was based on the reincarnation of a behaviour model, transcendent emulation. He did not assume he could discipline by striking him. Gerald did not like being called a fabulist, but he blamed himself for allowing matters to deteriorate to that level. There were new markets opening in Thailand. Gerald booked a business trip for two with an extended tour of the region, including the Great Wall of China.

"Your passport came in the mail, Price. You look like your finger was in an electrical outlet in your picture."

"Can I keep it?" he asked.

"No. It's best I hang on to it for now. I'll let you give it to the inspectors at the airports when we go on the trip."

"I'm not sure I want to go. You have business to do."

"You are my business. You'll help me."

Their flight was uneventful but protracted. Oddly enough, the longest delays had occurred on the North American leg of the journey. Price's arm and haunch still felt sensitive after receiving his shots. Dragging his hand baggage was not pleasant. At the time, most people, Gerald included, imagined South-East Asia as post-war debris. Although the fighting in Vietnam had ended at least fifteen years before, it was difficult to think that reconstruction under the Communists would have amounted to much more than the building of a few government offices, greyly appointed in cheap cinder block. Thailand was not Vietnam either before Dienbienphu or after the Tet Offensive. It had been more commercially developed and did not suffer the intensity of civil wars and foreign insurgency as did Cambodia or South Vietnam. At the Bangkok airport, they were greeted by what looked like a gang of greeters, hoisting Welcome signs with Gerald's name on them when he stepped through the Arrivals gate. Price and his grandfather were taken away in a large black Pontiac which accommodated both the visitors and the greeters.

His grandfather left Price in the hotel room by himself most of the day that coincided with his thirteenth birthday. The elevator either did not work or the elevator man was off-duty when he was not supposed to be. Price ran up and down the stairs from the fourth floor numerous times to pass the hours. The hotel was built in colonial times and bore distinctive European accents, like the exterior façade with its arches, balconies, fake columns and gargoyles. Many guests used the stairs to get to their rooms because of the unresponsiveness of the elevator. At night, Gerald took him to an American-style Thai restaurant that served a foreign hamburger on the children's menu.

To the taste, the hamburger was a mixture of animal tubing, tails, muscle and eggs. The patty only stayed together by being embedded in a glue of mustard on a half-crisp, half-wet bun. The cola had the fleeting flavour of used gum. The edge of the napkin was stained by a former soup.

"I want to go home," Price said as he played with the rubbery meat. "Everyone on the street looks at us. We stand out, don't we?"

"How about this. Business is finished. Tomorrow, we fly to China. The Forbidden City. One billion Chinese. Chinese food!"

Gerald talked so much about how closed China used to be, what a threat it posed, how big it was, that Price had to yawn defensively several times during their trip to Peking. Once there, Price had to admit the vastness of the main streets, the visual vacuum in the lack of passenger cars, the density of the crowds and markets, the presence everywhere of soldiers.

Gerald had a number of business opportunities in China he wanted to pursue for himself and businessmen who had asked him to follow up leads. This was the next land of opportunity where Western businesses were contracting out production of vats of chemicals for brand-name cosmetics, stained glass for church walls and fur hats for Hasidic Jews, board games and cutlery, designer clothing and instrument panels, all for one-fiftieth of the cost back home. Price imagined millions of Chinese workers with tens of millions of nimble fingers sequestered in massive catacombs with just enough light and bread, emotionless except for their enthusiasm for detail and the expectation of earning ten cents a day. The myth was that no project or plant manager could be trusted with quality or deadlines, and no inspector would ever exhaust all the bureaucratic regulations unless he was paid to go away. The sociology was not worthy of understanding but of exploiting at a risk. He thought Price would witness what this world was like for the experience and to make home life more endearing. Again he left Price alone for most of the afternoon at the hotel, trusting the English newspapers and books of crossword puzzles he had bought for him would keep him occupied.

At the downstairs restaurant, which was bordered with thickly padded furniture, Price sat at one of the spare wooden tables and sipped a poorly-flavored orange drink. At an adjoining table sat a man he recognized by his broad-rimmed hat: they had checked in at the same time. He was hunched over a bowl of thin soup. Price and the man acknowledged each other with a quick tilt of the brow. The man brought his bowl over to Price's table and introduced himself as a government advisor in town to attend a conference. His accent was European, maybe Spanish. At first Price thought he saw his eyes: they were just out of his sight below the edge of his brim.

He drew out his hand from under the table, extended a palm with five widely-spaced fingers to Price. Price looked at his large, welcoming limb, raised his own, and shook hands.

'I came with a little dog. You may have seen it yesterday at the registration desk," he said before bringing the spoonful of soup to his mouth. "I left the conference center for lunch. I found a small hole-in-the-wall restaurant on a side street I had wandered into. There was nothing on the menu I understood. The waiter motioned he would bring me something I would like. My dog was minding its own business on my lap, but the waiter took it to the back room, behind a curtain. I thought this was for sanitary reasons. Sanitation did not seem to be the outstanding feature of the place. The main course came after a number of appetizers."

He asked Price to slide over the salt. Price obliged.

"The meat tasted like a mixture of tough chicken and soft lamb. It took the time to finish off half the plate before I realized... I ate my own dog."

Price could not tell if the narrator was speaking out of despair. His voice gave no hint of it, until he dropped the spoon into the bowl, slapped the table hard enough to make the soup jump over the edges of the bowl and hissed into the little puddle under his forearm, "Bloody country." Price wanted to see the full expression on his face. He could not because the man seemed to intentionally tilt his hat brim over his eyes to avoid direct contact.

A uniformed man entered the restaurant, ostensibly looking for someone. He had one white blind eye.

"I have to go. That's my driver. There's hardly anyone on the road. And he likes to speed."

They spent two days on the tour bus, driving around the sites of Peking. On the third, they rented bicycles to complete their tour. Gerald had enough of cycling after half an hour. Price insisted on staying out longer. The bicycle was oversized, and had no gears. The seat was wide and accommodating. In the distant past, the tires had had white sidewalls. The chain, clotted with grease, had a leg guard.

"Stick around the hotel," said Gerald.

Price joined the flow of bike traffic down the main street. The traffic consisted of delivery trucks, scooters, bicycles and a few vans. At home, the same road space would not have been cobbled and would have been consumed almost exclusively by sedans. He had brought an apple and pastry with him, which he ate in a small park after an hour of leisurely pedaling. He walked his bicycle a bit farther, coming to what his pocket map showed as Tiananmen Square. Military trucks were pulling up, stopping just behind him. Since he had left his grandfather at the hotel, he sensed he was being watched, probably by his grandfather. There were such overwhelming waves of people all about him, whoever was following him was well hidden. It did not take much to hide. There were so many eyes.

Price was swept into the south corner of the Square by a push of shoeless runners. People lying on blankets on the ground shouted at him, waved their arms. Price found himself using his handle-bars as a shield.

Thousands had turned the Square into a massive campground. Blankets, banners, posters, clothing and human feces littered most of the area as if a strong wind re-arranged a marketplace off a back-street. Soldiers armed with rifles marched in groups through paths they made by kicking away water buckets and bedding material. About three hundred feet ahead, a group was doing aggressive calisthenics in bare feet, shouting whenever they clapped their hands overhead.

His grandfather had told him the government had to be very strict with its people because there are so many of them. Multiple bodies, multiple faces, endless opportunity to think divergent, non-conformist thoughts.

"You need a lot of police and a lot of rules to make sure a crowd doesn't become a riot."

He said everyone was poor. It didn't take much to start a stampede. Just one person screaming 'Fire!' Someone did scream, but it was not the people exercising in front of him. In fact, there was a lot of shouting coming from all directions in what appeared to be a coordinated cheerleading type sound-off. Price thought firecrackers were snapping. Something was happening behind him causing a surge in the crowd to advance. Yelping voices were broadcasting panic. Extremely thin dogs lost the ability to voice their barks. A bloodied woman fell over the front wheel of his bicycle. Just ahead, a teenager, squatting, spat into his open palms and with his hands, brushed away lint or invisible stains covering his velveteen pants. He repeated this obsessive activity, neither taking delight in nor acquiring a distaste for the routine in which he was trapped. Price was afraid he had become a cat.

An irregular line of soldiers far to his right shot at the people in front of them. A few soldiers were tackled from behind and beaten once on the ground. One of them was set on fire. Dark splashes of debris flew up from a wild, churning mass of people, as if a huge gathering of black birds had just been scattered. Two tanks moved forward at a slow rumble. People clambered on top like wasps over a target. The strong stench of gasoline and meat wafted.

Price was transfixed by the chaos, neither ducking nor falling to the ground as others around him were doing. His foreign status prevented his curiosity from crumbling into fear. A voice behind his ear, like the speaker in a department store, softly and persuasively announced: "Please follow me". It was audible above the agonized moaning and shrill tumult. A hand, at first gentle, then firm, fell on his hand perched on the handlebar, leading the bicycle and Price out of the Square. His guide was not Chinese; but his English instructions were accented. He was dressed in a white suit, white shirt, was tie-less and wore a hat. It was the man he had met at the hotel. Price though could not see his full face, because of his hat and the commotion.

"Do not look back or to the side. You will turn to salt if you look away from my back."

Which is what Price did. Within minutes, the inescapable clutter of chewed-up poles, pillows, sandals and blood had been left behind. Once past a phalanx of military vehicles, his guide hopped on his own bicycle, inviting Price to race him back to the hotel. Two loud explosions erupted behind them. Price was having difficulty keeping up with his racing partner.

Above, the sky-scape looked like a cheap painting by a sidewalk artist.

Small black birds dove at the gold-plated roof of the Forbidden City palace north of the Square. Beneath them, the multitudinous rooms in the Halls of Precious Clouds and Heavenly Purity, and Benevolence and Longevity hosted echoes, but no people. Shadows of the Ming dynasty took their vestiges of power and escaped by a back route as the troops took control of the mass of protesters beyond the walls. Around the City, bicyclists pedaled faster, fan and silk scarf hawkers shouted out their wares louder, cooks at hole-in-the-wall restaurants boiled their soups longer, government loudspeakers at major intersections coughed up new detours, old women on park benches looked more closely at the size of their feet. Bakers saw their bread going stale faster than usual.

When he ran into the hotel lobby, Gerald pulled him near by the forearm.

"We have to leave the country. Get packed pronto."

It was the first time Price had seen his grandfather upset to the extent of being almost out of control. He had stiffened his back. His eyes appeared watery, showing his age.

Price was silent. He said little during their long trip home. He was filled with awe and disgust. What was most disturbing was the stink and disorder in the Square. It had a historic floor plan very much like a library. The brutality of the clean-up was a logical step in the restoration of free access, aisles and the accepted way of life. During the military put-down, flocks of crows rained down spittle on the crowds as a cleanser.

On the airplane, with some foresight, Price recorded his impressions in the empty spaces in the many maps his grandfather had gathered for the trip. His writings filled up the China

Sea, the Indian Ocean, Tibet and Siberia. In some places, he would make little drawings of his bicycle, boxy tanks, squares.

Once home, he continued to write; this time though, he ran his impressions through the typewriter. When he wore out the black length of the typewriter ribbon, he flipped onto the red side so that the last part of his memoir was typed in red ink.

Gerald was impressed with the diary of their journey. With Price's consent he showed it to friends, one of whom published books for juveniles. The events described had such resonating political and social currency, the publisher worked out a publishing arrangement with Gerald to format and entitle the work "Journey to a Forbidden Land". The book was an instant hit, published under a pseudonym Price chose, Jacky Little. It went through three rapid printings until a newspaper columnist suggested the Red Chinese government was buying up large quantities for propaganda purposes to emphasize no massacre had occurred. Within weeks after that column appeared, the work was being remaindered in many of the franchise book stores.

Price was oblivious to the success of the book and to the impressive royalties Gerald had received and placed in trust for him. Price was in a second-hand book store to buy a thesaurus when he spotted dozens of copies of the volume in a remainder bin. He thought the books looked very comfortable in a casual pile in the wire mesh bin, and hoped no one would disturb it.

"It feels like so long ago," Price told Gerald, showing him the thesaurus. "I still have bad dreams about what happened."

"You can't stop dreams from coming. If they want to come, they will. You know that story about me in the airplane..."

"Grandpa, I'm too old to hear that. Besides, it wasn't even a story."

"I was a junior navigator during the Second World War. I was in an airplane flying over occupied Poland."

Price interrupted: "And the airplane made lots of noise."

"We flew reconnaissance missions over what looked like a little city. It was the Auschwitz Birkenau concentration camp that was killing civilians. We took a lot of pictures from the air. There were rows and rows of houses or barracks. Like a little city full of people who were only there to die. And you're right. Nothing happened. We didn't drop bombs on the railroad lines. We didn't shoot up the place where they burned people. We brought back our pictures. The place was smartly laid out. Someone thought a long time how to build that place. And they did. a few weeks later, I handed a letter to my superior officer saying I wanted to go back and bomb the place. I got no answer. I got nothing but a real kick in the stomach when I saw the newsreels once the camps were liberated.

A few years later, I was in an airplane again. Same job, same uniform, but a little bit older. We flew over the jungles in Korea and dropped a lot of bombs. There was not pattern on the ground. Just trees and empty green spaces. Who knows who we hit."

Price listened with no particular image in mind other than that of a military uniform, khaki.

"It's hard to find evil if it's hiding. It's hard to look for it if you don't want to find it. The world's not predictable. You would assume that if everything is under someone's control, that person would have no reason to hurt anyone. It's not true. Just because everything is neatly laid out doesn't mean it's a sign for the good."

Price said he would be afraid of a jungle.

"Price, there are no jungles in China."

"Those students were breaking the law."

"Why do your dreams bother you?"

"I don't know... The noise, the smells. I wasn't ready."

Chapter 7

Price in Jail

Price was arrested again for setting fire to a disorderly pile of picket signs left on the curb outside the school by striking maintenance workers. The strike had already begun curtailing the length of the school day, causing parents enormous re-scheduling problems with child pick-up. During lunch hour, Price shouted at the strikers to go away and give him back his school. While waiting for his car-pool, he bought a lighter from a smoker in a higher grade, and lit the signs.

He felt no joy in the process of destruction even if it was necessary. One of the strikers called him a punk while another kicked him in the shin. Price was about to spit back. He realized spittle conveyed no moral lesson the striker could take away with him.

"Leave my school alone."

Price's last arrest came not long after the bonfire. Television broadcast images of mobs tearing down the Wall separating East and West Berlin. Youths picked away at the blocks of cement with sledge hammers, baseball bats, and tire irons.

His home-room teacher brought to class a newspaper which had a front-page photo of a group Iwo Jima-style atop part of the Wall hoisting or pulling in a concerted tug-of-war.

"A day in history. The Iron Curtain is coming down," announced his teacher wearing an epauletted blouse and pleated skirt.

While many of his classmates still grappled with the image of an iron curtain, he stood to solemnly say, "Barbarians are destroying the Wall".

"What do you mean, Price?" his teacher asked.

"They have no beards, but they are destroyers."

"What are you saying, Price? Who are the barbarians?"

Price could not contain himself. Price saw the issue as an act of frenzied disorder, defying a massive Dewey Decimal System that kept everyone in place. He could not understand it except to acknowledge that chaos is the result of muddled thinking. Once the Wall came down, didn't these Germans know there was cheap meat in the West and expensive meat in the East, two price tags on the same item?

He walked out of the room just as the end-of-the-day bell sounded. Once home, he ran around the neighborhood and his own back yard gathering bricks, patio stones, and rocks. By the evening, he had erected a wall of debris six feet high and equally wide on the curb with the help of the kids on the block who were fascinated with Price's initiative.

The wall projected from the curb part way toward the median line of the street. Most drivers easily swerved around the construction even though it came up without warning. One driver, lulled by nightfall, smashed his car into it, demolishing the wall and breaking his grill, headlights, hood and nose.

The event brought out the police and eventually the media. The reporters thought initially that Price was re-enacting the destruction of the Wall. They could not understand the large banner that read: *Don't eat your own dog!* When they realized he was trying to reconstruct it, the makings of a greater story emerged. Two newspaper columns suggested there was a fifth column in suburbia. Price's remarks in class were leaked by his previously never-noticed teacher. Those comments fed the rumour that East German spies had known about the possible fall of their government in advance, and had slipped into North America to get away from the revenge of the masses. The columns were accompanied by stills of Price lifted from school pictures.

Gerald was livid when he first saw one of the stories. His lawyer demanded an immediate retraction from the papers which they at first refused to do. Together, they later paid eight hundred thousand dollars for insinuating Price and his family were spies.

The guards at the youth correctional facility were each over eighty-five years old. Sometimes, they would watch television together after work hours, although hearing the audio was problematic. Many preferred playing cards, or an abridged version of bingo that gave bonus points for each hit. The warden had just reached eighty. She liked to sleep sitting up on the couch in the games room with her co-workers.

No inmate or guest had ever escaped from the experimental institution because he theoretically wanted to be there. *"This is not a jail"* read the motto on the banner hung on the wall. The same inscription was printed on the buttons the guards wore on their blazers instead of badges. It was not the spryness but the disguised frailty of the guards that earned the respect of the young guests, most of whom had never seen a grandparent, or natural parent for that matter. No-one on staff was incontinent, forgetful, partially blind, thoroughly deaf, or smelled, any of which traits would have made them exploitable. Their ability to discipline was based on disapproving facial expressions rather than a strong arm. If any inmate stepped out of line, he knew in his worst nightmare his punishment would be waking up in a damp bed, suffering from wrinkled skin, brown skin spots and an impossible realization that he had aged fifty years overnight.

Price did not think he could last another day in the place. The building and mattresses were so old. Every one in authority was so old. The tennis racquets were warped and made of wood, not metal. The softball stitching was unraveling. Although activities started punctually, there were many extended periods of dead time during the day. The boys had to sit in the dining hall usually for a half hour after they had eaten their meal, because the seniors were still on their soup. Whenever they went on outings, sitting time on the bus before traveling was extended, as was sitting and waiting before disembarking. The pace could not have been more ill-suited for the inmates, no better suited for the seniors. The institution was there to slow down the inmates' metabolism.

Harry Souply as a teenager did not like his name. His school principal called him ShewFly. His homeroom teacher Mrs. Spunk took to calling him Henry after her husband, as did his peers.

Years before, Harry had rented a room in the home of an old woman, using his pseudonym. His landlady suffered a mild stroke shortly after Harry's arrival. Her children, who lived far away, were happy to have Harry, known as Henry, stay in the house during her convalescence in a care facility. With the passage of time, though, her son en route from visiting his mother, stopped by the house to speak with him.

"You're not paying rent, are you, Henry?" he said as he paced the living room, quickly taking stock of the furnishings.

"I'm looking after the house," Harry answered proficiently.

"And you're living in it," the son said with a stern directness.

"Saving you the cost of watching it and losing your insurance."

"Why don't we do this: my mother is not going to come back. She can't live on her own. I'm going to put it up for sale next month and clean it out. So please make arrangements to leave in the next couple of weeks."

"You're Dick from California. Your pictures are all over this living room."

During the following week, Harry hoarded. Under his bed, he stored most of the canned foods he found in the kitchen pantry. On his night table, he placed the landlady's toaster oven, wrapped in his yellow nylon windbreaker. The bread box now served as a support for his television set. The iron and the dishes were stored inside the microwave.

After three weeks of inertia by Harry, the son called from California, then had the water turned off. Harry called the utility several times to complain of lack of water for the old woman's bath, until the water was restored. Same with the electric power. Same with the telephones. Once the locks on the doors were changed overnight, Harry crawled in and out of the basement windows. He would not be dislodged and so limited his departures. When he did go outside, he made sure the television and lights in the main rooms were on.

Notes slipped under the door and posted on some windows, invariably proclaimed "*Get Out*". The police would not assist in his eviction without a court order, which would have taken time. Two policemen did stop by once to walk the perimeter of the house when they noticed police tape stapled across the front door.

When plumbers arrived to remove all the toilets in the house, Harry called Dick in California to offer to buy the house, cash down, closing in one week. The son agreed, even though the price was far below market. Although the plumbers were paid for their time, they had hoped to take away the four ample white porcelain toilet bowls which they were going to use to grow cucumbers in once installed in their sun porches.

Within the month, Harry sold the house at a profit. Emboldened by his success, Harry established a pattern. He purchased and sold five successive houses all over the city within a two year period in the same way, more than doubling the money his father-in-law had long before given him. Each time, he ferreted out a vulnerable senior, and aggravated a distant family member.

Except the next time. He had managed to have his landlady change her will to leave him all her savings. When she took ill and was removed to the hospital, he holed up in the house until the daughter came to inspect the very home she had lived in as a child. She told Harry that her mother had talked about him, how comforting it was to have someone else to interact with in a big lonely house.

"She died last night, Henry."

"I am shocked. She looked so well over the weekend before she went. It was her birthday. I bought her a little cake a few days ago," he said.

"She told me. It was so sweet of you, Henry. All I could do for my mother was to call long-distance."

Then Harry said: "You should know something. Here's her new will". The daughter mechanically took the document. Rapidly coming to see what was going on, she remained seated on the couch, reflecting on a blur of options. He could have been a Raskolnikov bent on eliminating her mother.

"If you're thinking of selling the house, I would buy it off your hands... Do you hear what I'm saying?" Harry said helpfully.

She listened and nodded. As she stood, she opened her purse, withdrawing from it a small revolver.

"Want to die?" she said.

Harry showed her his palms in self-defense. He tore up the will at the coffee table. She told him to leave the house immediately.

"I'm not wearing shoes," Harry was being practical.

"You won't need shoes if you're dead," she said, concerned that he might think she was holding a toy.

A cab happened to be traveling down the street. The cabbie was lucky to pick up a fare to the airport without a dispatcher.

Visitors were rare in the detention facility. Once a juvenile was sent away, the family was not in a hurry to see the child again. Price had been in and out for periods of weeks since he torched the picket signs. When Napanee refused to let his social worker into the house for a scheduled meeting, Price was incarcerated for three months on his fourteenth birthday. The social worker would not accept as an excuse Napanee's insistence that she was putting blond highlights into her mother's hair in the living room.

"Happy birthday, Price," the man said over the visitor's table. He did not fidget, so he seemed to be a person in authority. On the other hand, he was too well dressed and confidently eager to be an official. Since Price could not place him or explain his enthusiasm, he thought the visitor must be a pedophile or lost.

"Who are you?"

"My name is Harry Souply. Your name is Price Souply" he said, as if putting order to the world.

"First name is right. Last name is not," Price said as he rose to leave. The less he engaged him in conversation, the better.

"Sit, sit. You're mother is Napanee DeMann... I'm the father you never saw. Souply, De Mann. Supply and demand?"

Up to that point, Price was prepared for a deviant social worker who had gone through his files, but not this. It may have been the biggest lie anyone had dared tell him. He was intrigued enough to court with disappointment. Why would he need a father now in any event? Returning to his chair, he analyzed Harry's face. His own face had changed so much with puberty, he had little direction in finding some affinity. A white fog floated over Harry's eyes, cheeks and chin. Visibility was poor below his father's baseball cap. Harry did not seem to be concerned about anyone around him. That was a sign he was telling the truth.

"Let's say you're right. Let's say you're wrong. What do you want?" Price said, emotionless.

The discordance of the moment was heightened by the music coming out of the record player in the visitors' hall. An LP featuring Jingle Bells and other seasonal ditties backed up by bells and the clip-clop of horses, found its way to the turntable amid a donated selection of albums on the same theme. This July day was exceptionally cold, yet not frosty enough to swing to the beat of Silent Night. Did people like Mitch Miller and his choir? And if so, why would they give away his albums?

"I brought you something to prove I'm your father. You know what this is? A word processor." Harry patted the box on the floor next to his leg but out of Price's line of vision. Sensing that he had caught Price's attention, Harry took a keyboard and monitor out of the box that had been taped around several times. Once they were on the table, he pushed the keyboard over to Price's hands.

"You plug it in. You type, erase, save, all without paper."

"I know what a computer is..."

"A personal computer, you mean. Listen, Price. This is special."

"Why is it special?" Price asked, looking at the profile of the screen.

"I stole it," Harry said proudly.

Price looked more closely at the keyboard. For the next few minutes, Price listened to Harry's most recent exploits as a con man. He had convinced a computer dealer to take an uncertified cheque, after floating a story that he worked for a police agency shopping for thirty new computers.

"I told him if the machine was powerful enough, and the feel was good, I would be back for more. I left him the card of an accountant I had found pinned to a supermarket bulletin board. I hear you're in the same line of business."

"Big mistake. I don't steal. That's your living." Price became concerned about having his fingerprints on the keyboard.

"Why do you hurt people, Price?" Harry asked, looking for a connection.

"Are you a shrink? That's the type of question a shrink would ask."

Harry sat back meaningfully. "I don't want to understand you. I want to understand me. I did the same thing when I was your age. Sounds like it's genetic. What I'm saying is that whatever reason you think you have for doing your thing, it's not. You're doing it because I did it. We're working with the same material." Harry thought he had made the point well, but found little immediate reaction.

Price scanned Harry's face. Behind him, a guard who had been doing crossword puzzles by the window got up to change the record. The Bing Crosby Special started off with an orchestral flourish highlighting what a wonderful day it was.

"Why do I have to be like you. I don't have to. You're nobody to me."

"What are you talking about? I'm rich because of what I do and how I do it. Price, I know you're leaving this place next month. I'm glad I caught you before you got out. I want you to come with me. Live with me."

That was a sign Harry was indeed a deviant who had done his homework on his personal information.

"Mom is expecting me home. What's Mom's name again? What colour hair does she have?"

"Napanee. Blond. You still live at your grandparents' house. Grandpa's name is Gerald. He hates me but would prefer to see me hurt instead of dead."

"Are you a molester or something? What do you want from me, even if you're my father?"

"You're a small-time punk who always gets caught. Sounds like you need some parental guidance."

"What? You're going to teach me how to be a big-time crook?"

A white-haired guard came over to tell Harry visiting was almost over. She smelled of cedar closet. She told him he could not leave his gift with Price. There were freshly baked muffins for visitors on their way out.

"I used to like closing time. All the annoying people would have to leave. Mom could cry like a leaky tap."

"Are you worried about what she would say if you came with me?" Harry asked. He wasn't sure what would work to convince him.

"Maybe I'm more worried about myself."

"How is she? I haven't seen her since I left," Harry said, reaching into his pocket.

"You ask her."

"Price, here's a wedding picture I bet you never saw. Me and Mom. You keep it. See you."

Harry did leave him another gift, a small match box, which was undetected by the guard. He gave it to Price palm-to-palm in their last handshake.

Back in his room, Price sat down at his desk, his elbows touching the stacks of department store catalogues Napanee had brought him to read. Harry was gone and Price was glad because he now had to decide whether to feel disturbed, enraged, fulfilled, amused or disinterested. The sandy side of the match box was chafing his leg. Removing it, he noticed a telephone number written in black ink across its logo. There were no matches inside, because it did not matter. What looked like a black ball suddenly unfolded its legs. A sizeable spider clambered out of the box, over his startled hand, to the floor, going directly into the corner of the room where it rolled up into a ball again. Price went after it with one of the catalogues. He did not want to kill it, just flip if out of the corner and out the open window. The spider contracted into a tighter ball, making it difficult for Price to maneuver the cover of the catalogue under it.

Price recognized that the spider had what he figured was intelligence. A fly was fast but half-minded. A mosquito was fast and suicidal. A butterfly was slow and fastidious. Bees were heavy and arrogant. This spider knew about the safety of corners. It sensed not only Price's presence, but also his intent. Price tried lifting it with the eraser tip of a pencil, to no effect. He finally succeeded by using a plasticized book mark. The spider did not resist being flicked out on the ledge. It lowered itself by a thread, beginning a leisurely rappel down the wall.

The door to his room swung open. No-one was there except a gust. Most importantly, Harry was not there. It opened the way the front cover of a text book can be flipped open with the spring action of the thumb under the index finger. It opened like eyelids to a bright light. He was a large inmate in a large textbook. The spider was a period in a sentence Price had dislocated, throwing off the meaning of the entire text. Why did he need a father? The front cover was angry because it no longer reflected the context left in shambles by a rappelling spider. Price took control by shutting the door but not locking it. If it was still dissatisfied, it could open itself.

Napanee had not noticed Price was not at home. After returning from an overseas trip, her father asked if she had picked him up from the institution weeks before. She was at a loss. Napanee was a busy woman. Her work ate up most of her day. She was a product tester right there in the home or the back yard or the garage. Her mother was her best assistant. Consumer magazines sent her products to use, compare and keep, like five different models of grills, or sewing machines, or video players. After one use and the submission of her results, her mother would sell the items through a network of buyers she had established. Napanee came highly recommended by her shopping circles, including the former manager of the store where she used to work.

Some of the items she kept for her father's use. The golf cart, the roto-tiller, the speaker system. Some she left for her mother, like the juicer and electric steak-knife. She built up an impressive collection of video games and play equipment for Price.

The call came a day after Gerald discovered Price was not home. Napanee had difficulty realizing Harry was at the other end of the line: his voice was out of place. Only an hour before, she had found a sock missing for months curled behind the dryer. She spoke with mixed feelings.

"You were hiding behind a dryer. Full of lint, Harry." She imagined he still looked as he did years before, and was in fact lounging in front of the television in the den."

"What are you talking about, Napanee?"

"Now you think I'll take you back. I threw out that sock, because I threw out the other one a long time ago. We can never make a pair again."

"I don't want you to take me back, Napanee. If you're looking for Price, he's with me." Harry paused for a reaction.

"Well, bring him back when you're finished."

"I'm never bringing him back. He's mine now," Harry asserted.

"Tell him he's in big trouble. What do you want with him? Where are you?"

"If you want him back, tell your father it'll cost him. Price came with me voluntarily. If you want him back, I'm going to have to tell him it's better at your place. I can't stand to disappoint him after he's been clinging to me. That'll cost fifty thousand. I'll call tomorrow after nine."

"Harry, it's like talking to a stranger. I never knew you, you know. I haven't thought about you all these years."

"Price is my son. I'm entitled to trade him."

"How do you know he's yours, Harry? How do you know that?"

Price, who had been pacing behind his father, suddenly pulled the phone from Harry's hand.

"Mom, I'm staying with my father. He really is my father. He gave me a 386 computer. I've been on it ever since I got here. What a machine!"

Napanee took the cue and whispered: "I'll get accessories that double the speed. It's all speed, you know."

"I see that," Price acknowledged.

That night, Price stole Harry's wallet while he slept. He caught the eleven thirty bus and was home by two in the morning. When Harry awoke, Gerald was standing over him, in the company of three men, all holding axe handles. Gerald cautioned him not to move. One of the men moved around the house setting fire to the couch, punching in the television set, pouring cement down the kitchen drain and the toilets, and spray painting the carpeting.

Chapter 8

Love Comes Home

The idea of Harry, not Harry himself, disturbed her. His name made no appearance in her vocabulary. The formation of her words, the pressure of her tongue on her upper palate, the puckering of her lips in order to express her basic needs or keep a searing secret did not depend on him, his name, his body image, his odour, his itch to be somewhere else when there was nowhere else. Even when she said 'hurry', she did not think of Harry. She never said 'harried' or 'hark' or harlot', so the issue never arose in those cases. Hungry, Hungary, Harold, Harrod, hardy, harness: none of the words were evocative. She had never heard the song I'm just wild about Harry.

Why would anyone be wild about Harry, or a Harry in general? If wild meant savage, was it realistic to think no person could turn savage or unfettered because of another. Love might stimulate creativity. Could it also turn a smile to a snarl, or a vegetarian into a meat-eater? Anyway, the point was that a Harry could not bring about a night-to-day revision of character or attitude. Nothing could, except for the extreme shock of too much money or long-term imprisonment in jail located near the Equator. That's when change is possible or even probable.

Sheep recognize hundreds of sheep faces. They have to in order to live tolerably in flocks, rubbing by each other's wool by accident or by design. We see them as sweaters or lamb chops, faceless, unidentifiable individually unless the washed cardigan pills after a laundry. Napanee could not pick him out of a flock of Harrys. Black sheep, white sheep, he did not have any wool. Not even steel wool, resting in a clump by the faucet in a puddle of rust.

She had no need of him. She had her family, her home. Loneliness was not an issue. Neither was finding a role or fulfillment. Maybe it was peer review, peer talk. Napanee did not need a man. She needed to express that she truly had no room in her busy life for a man. She had school girlfriends she had grown up with and who now worked for her. They were like her, quickly married and divorced, who enjoyed teasing each other. Perhaps it was a recent comment one had made and the other had confirmed: Napanee was sagging. Maybe it was the idea of Harry, the fact of intrusion, unchanging opportunism, the never-ending return of an undesirable taste, or buzz of a fast horsefly that always annoys.

Her friend Cheryl, who had always said she had gotten pregnant at Woodstock, in fact had not. Loose language was her handicap. As she got older and had more children, she questioned whether she had been to Woodstock at all or had started on the way and given up in bad traffic. Woodstock actually meant the idea of Woodstock. Woodstock appears on the map of Vermont and New York, and countless other places. What she meant was that she got pregnant in any small town, not necessarily in a farmer's field surrounded by billions of disoriented tee-shirts, manipulative older men, hawkers, psy-chos, pick-pockets and comfortable white families looking for a nice place to picnic and run away from in-laws. Getting preg-nant was like being in a field because it felt like being bitten by a deranged horse fly. She could feel conception. She detested her husband that much.

When she said Napanee was sagging, she meant very slightly lop-sided or minimally off-kilter. From the back, the slope of one shoulder was less pronounced than that of the other. It all depended on the angle of perception. So Cheryl would say, with exaggerated lip movement when she wanted to emphasize a point to Napanee, the idea of Woodstock was like the idea of Harry. The object of the idea was history, un-real, tenuous. The idea itself only had life if someone thought about it.

Napanee had no insight into the metaphor Cheryl had used. Nothing was like Harry because he no longer existed. There could not be a truism brought to greater clarity through a metaphor based on Harry. It would be like saying the moon is as yellow as molecule's belly. The equal signs in an algebraic equation were there not merely for convenience: they con-nected things that had a previous relationship, or should have one. She told Cheryl to shut up because she was talking too much and giving her a headache.

Sagging gave Napanee no choice. She bought a new ward-robe one size smaller, and foundation garments much smaller. She asked her mother at least twice a day if she was beautiful; the reply inevitably being: "My daughter will always be beau-tiful", the counter-reply being: "Like you, Mommy."

They meant everything they said to each other. Not that any of it was true. It did not have to be, as long as it was mean-ingful. They probably had never said anything truthful. All of it was innocuous, consistent and terribly important because it hit home and remained.

"Be honest, what about these earrings, Cheryl?"

"You have smallish ears. The earrings are too big."

"What do you mean, smallish?"

"Guys like smaller ears." I look like a freak with my big lobes."

"What guys like smaller ears?"

"Same guys that like small feet. Walk into a room full of men. They look at your feet and ears."

"Nothing else."

"I'm talking about what they really go for."

They picked the nits out of each other's sentences. They cherished the juicy words, remembered them as comforting and timely. Not only were they each beautiful, and forever so, they were, historically speaking, the most beautiful in any progressive civilization.

Napanee and Cheryl joined a swing-dancing club. Most of the décor of the studio, the instructor's outfit and the dancing was inspired by the 1950s. Cheryl's plump of hair was well suited to the decor. They had to be coaxed into coming onto the centre of the studio floor and letting go of their purses. They did have the sense to bring tennis shoes. The instructor gave them elastic-waist skirts that flared up and out when they spun around, and clung to their legs like a collapsed parachute when they stopped.

They were each musical, had a natural rhythmic body sway that made them alluring dance candidates. Dance was second nature, which they rarely enjoyed because it made no practical sense. Walking made sense, although it was too mundane to receive any notice.

After two evening sessions, they both realized they were a few years too old for the energy required to keep up with the men. They weren't even men. Men did not move that quickly, or did not dare to. These were adolescents, maybe thirty years old at most, wagging their feet on their heels while waiting for their partner to end the spin and jump on and off their knees as the saxophone solo directed them. Cheryl had a problem with the step-by-step approach because her partner pressed his whole body against the back of hers too firmly and too longingly, and held her across the chest too vividly for her imagination. She even called him a pervert and told him to let go. He asked if she preferred to fall instead of being held securely. She told him to grab someone else. Napanee did not seem to have the same problem. In fact, she thought her partner was too wimpish and would easily let her injure herself before he would take the fall.

"Either you're going to dance with me or you're not."

Her partner complained she was not holding his hand properly.

"You're hands are sweaty. I'll hold your fingers. Why don't you wipe your palms or wear gloves or something," Napanee snapped back.

"Complaining is not allowed here. And you can't cherry-pick partners."

"I'll do what I want. And you are not what I want," Napanee said as she gave him the back of her right hand.

They then joined a tango club where Cheryl's hair was a liability. Dancing is a wave. A rush of water is the melting place of rolls and streams, fluid curls and trapped air. No wave is awkward or mis-stepped. Cheryl did not get it. Two dancers are part of the same wave by dint of their movement. Bad dancing means more debris, loose spurts of water, something that is never elevated to the level of a wave of wind or ultimately, a wave of sound. She thought the dance was immoral.

The immorality in two people dancing lies in the incongruity of their mutual expectations. If one looked to be moved instead of moving, while the other is confused by the message of movement, the morality of their partnership is questionable.

Cheryl could not afford to dance without Napanee's support and not because she did not know the steps. She was extremely agile, even athletic. She could not fathom why she had to fall victim to a rhythmic beat she recognized, and why she had to admit to a complete stranger she could, if she wanted to, generate a wave that could roll over most natural barriers. Her mistake lay in her own definition of privacy.

The instructor clapped out a beat with two hollow cylinders. His beat seemed to be slightly faster than that of the recorded music, or maybe it was simply more piercing. Cheryl did not think she needed it. In fact, it was irritating. When she eyed the instructor, he took her stare to mean total satisfaction. Bowing to her, he warmly reciprocated by clapping more energetically.

The male dancing partners were plentiful and intense, although considerably shorter once the women put on their high-heeled dancing shoes. They wore casual street clothes. One wore a business suit complete with tie and cuff links. Another sported a cummerbund across his waist and tuxedo pants. While there was no consistent intensity in their clothing, there was in their pursed lips, trimmed moustaches, or in the case of one dancer, his chic long side-burns. It did not matter: the men were made of cardboard, their hands plastic gloves. Their only personality was based on the fear of being injured while dancing, and being rejected while not dancing.

Napanee would have preferred that Cheryl not stick so closely to her during the sessions. She was like a back-up Flamenco guitarist to Napanee's lead.

"Go talk to your partner. You're base-sticking to me."

Cheryl stared at her for a moment, smarting from the reproach. She was going to say the same thing about Napanee. She was about to cry.

"I'm afraid of him. He speaks bad English."

"Unless he has bad breath, it doesn't matter what language he speaks."

"He speaks bad English. I don't think he speaks any other language."

Tango as a social experience was also short-lived. They were not allowed to dance in their tennis shoes. Their skirts had to be tighter, although it was preferable they wore dresses. Napanee's dance partner was an older gentleman, seemed to be cultured: he had a light touch, spoke little and used the raising of his eyebrows to signal his enjoyment of their dance. Cheryl's partner, according to her, spent most of the dance searching for the outlines of the bra strap at her back.

'He's just looking for a place to put his hand", Napanee suggested.

"You bet Napanee. Next time I'm going to wear a bullet-proof vest."

"Okay, test him. Next time don't wear a bra. See what he does."

"I'll have to bring a switch blade with me if I did that."

Napanee suspected Cheryl had issues she did not have. She was a liability. Not that she was bad looking or could not present well. She just slowed her down. Cheryl though was a companion, and for that she was thankful.

Friendship has its limits. A good friend is not necessarily a good teacher, a vibrant cheerleader, a strong moral compass, or a decent listener. A friend just happens to be there most of the time when being there has its uses. Napanee could not think of doing things without Cheryl, in the same way that family was not the same without the people she knew as family. Although not always.

In her despair, she drove toward Cheryl's house, even though it was late. A block away, she drove past a parked car and thought the woman on the passenger side was Cheryl. She had not noticed who was sitting in the driver's seat. Thinking it strange, she circled the block and slowly drove past the parked car. Whoever was the driver now had his arm around Cheryl's neck and was moving to kiss her. Napanee circled one more time and confirmed they were kissing.

She drove to Cheryl's house, coming to a stop just before her lawn. Napanee called the house number. Her husband answered.

"What are you doing at home?"

"This is where I live Napanee."

"I mean, you're home while your wife is having an affair. Doesn't that bother you?"

"Is this a public service announcement?"

"I thought you should know."

"Why don't you tell Cheryl?"

"I would but she's busy down the street."

"That's interesting. She's also standing next to me as I hang up the curtains."

As soon as Cheryl came on the line, Napanee let out a laugh.

"Your husband's weird. I wouldn't trust him."

"That's what I've been telling you," Cheryl said.

The reason Cheryl was irritated had less to do with dancing than with a date. It was something she could not reveal to Napanee because she could not bring herself to acknowledge what she did.

On her way to the dance studio, Cheryl had left home early to drop off a sweater at her former neighbour's house. Once there, her neighbour introduced her to a cousin, a single male, who was visiting the city. Cheryl obliged by agreeing to drive him downtown, show him where the sites were and have a quick coffee before moving on to meeting Napanee.

Cheryl thought her guest took an immediate interest in her. In the car, he asked polite questions about the community, wondered about her relationship with his cousin, and went so far as asking if she was happy living where she was. Cheryl thought he was diplomatically warming up to her. She could tell he was only half listening to her when she pointed out the tourist sites. She noticed she hid her wedding band finger under the rim of the steering wheel as she drove. Once they parked in front of a car, she slipped her band into her coat pocket.

They sat directly across from each other over steaming cups. He waited for her to stop chattering, something she was self-conscious about. Cheryl had no idea what to say. She was too flattered to think straight.

"You have a lot of wrinkles around your eyes. Is that from the sun," she asked.

Before he could answer, she said he had many pores on his nose and asked if he was over sixty.

He was taken aback. Cheryl asked if he wanted to see anything specific in the city. He thanked her for her time and said he would remember her.

Without telling Cheryl, Napanee started going to office furniture auctions one evening a week in her smaller-sized outfits. Why should she tell her? Their commonality of interests was not all-inclusive. Just because Cheryl confided in her some of the intimacies spoken by her husband, that was no reason to lead her into her own secret desires. They both knew each was using the other, like the back scratcher and the back. One had a function, the other a need. What was wrong with that? Besides, there would be something new to talk about once everything had settled, a novel point raised by the way, totally unexpected and very refreshing to their relationship.

Napanee met a number of one-man operators looking to furnish the basement office. Most were in a hurry and had no intention of explaining to her what a good deal looked like, for fear of being manipulated out of it themselves. Except for one, who reluctantly admitted his name was Jeff. Being a novice and not in a hurry, Jeff was ready to chitchat with her. She had to prod him into a date to scout out another auction in the coming week.

He asked her no intrusive questions, spoke politely and expressed gratitude. She taught him what she knew about furniture quality and cost price. During the preview of the next auction they attended together, she took his hand and pulled him to see a genuine wood workstation. Although they missed the bid on the item, she asked if he had minded her pulling him around. Later, she surprised herself by asking him if he would call her.

Why did she surprise herself? She looked for the obvious reason, which was that she admittedly needed someone who was not dependent on her. She needed someone to whom she could explain herself as a peer. She loved Cheryl although she had her limitations. Put a better way to herself, she was tired of assuming she was always right. None of this made any sense to her. She just wanted to see Jeff again for the same reason she did not want to miss a bargain.

He did call during the week in the morning to see if they could have supper together. Napanee coyly consulted her agenda until she said yes. Jeff said he would pick her up by foot: he would walk the six miles to her house for the exercise. Besides, he did not like driving in the city. When he arrived at the door, she was surprised he had been serious, so surprised, she called Cheryl while he waited to tell her he was car-less.

"Do you want to walk to the restaurant?" Napanee laughed.

"If you put on your running shoes, I would," Jeff said.

Napanee did not know what to think. They drove to supper in her car, and she later dropped him off in front of his apartment. She felt the evening had gone well except for the fact that she did most of the talking and that he did not seem to share the same excitement she did in whatever topic she raised. Maybe he thought her talk was inconsequential, or even worse, silly. Maybe a middle-of-the-week supper was not a good idea to start with.

But her mind raced and brought him into the race. From week to week, they would meet for coffee, for inline skating, for a museum tour, for a movie. He made no demands and never called without asking if she would take his call. His politeness, his hinting but not expressing, his reticence to initiate, his respectability, washed over her, flooded her without giving her the time or ability to cling to anything secure.

"You're not saying anything, Jeff."

"I thought I just gave you the low-down of my day."

"Not much to it."

"It was peaceful, Napanee."

"I'm used to people talking without stopping. You know, no dead air in the conversation."

"Like on the radio."

"Yes."

"I find it hard to talk non-stop. I can breathe non-stop. Talking…?"

Napanee was not happy. Things that ordinarily mattered to her, like the weather and her outfit, her credit limit and credit balance, coupons and air-mile points, lost their sharpness, the clarity that made them stick in her mind. He became installed in her head like a big freezer or couch too bulky for a room. What should she get him? What should she do for him? What should she say to him? Those were the pre-occupying questions. No rudder, no keel, no steering wheel, no weather vane: there was nothing to direct or guide her outside her usual pattern.

Her normal impulse to talk quickly, wrap herself in anti-perspirant, avoid prolonged contact with others, socialize through a quick smile and maybe a soft body-check in a line, was low in voltage. Instead of reaching for the sales circulars, she began to worry about world events, albeit in a blurred way, asking herself why foreign people hated other foreign people, what Jeff would say about them.

Napanee read through an illustrated encyclopedia she picked up at a supermarket. The pictures were more alluring than the brief articles. She could not distinguish between the ancient Romans and the ancient Greeks. All the modern African countries had had several name changes in their recent history. Who could figure out where anything was and what the capitals were now called. Was there a difference between DNA and a gene?

Before getting off a chair, she would ask what of any interest could she say to him once she was standing. It made her uncomfortable, unhappy her discomfort followed her through snack meals and bedtime. Her nightmares depicted white powdered donuts turning into frogs in the box, her car melting on the driveway. Nothing made sense. She was afraid he would walk away from her.

He was a product without a price tag. She could not tell whether he was valuable or valueless, yet she could not let him go, nor could she haggle, until she could not bear it.

"Jeff, I have to know something."

"What is it?"

"You're too much of a gentleman to do anything more that hold my hand tightly, sometimes really tight… Do you feel anything for me?"

Jeff said he was glad to have this conversation, although he did not answer her question.

"I mean, I dream about you. I talk to you while I'm walking to my car."

"Napanee, I don't do that. I do think of you enough to call you."

"Do you feel, Jeff, not think?" Her impatience almost brought her to the point of telling him she did not like his sweater. As a token of endearment, her thoughts turned to hiring a woman to knit him a cardigan, one with bulk, colour, and lots of ribbing.

Jeff paused before responding, shifting his coffee cup to the side. He spoke methodically, slightly slower than usual so that she would not find him ambiguous.

"There is something about me you should know Napanee."

"What…you're gay? Married?"

"No. You're off in the wrong direction. First of all, we are very different types of people. What I find interesting in you is the drive you have. I have never seen someone so attracted to detail with such fascination."

"This is a compliment I hope. You're saying I'm fascinating?" She could feel herself fidgeting. She could no longer smell the perfume on her wrists.

"Anyway, that's not what I really wanted to tell you. I have a problem you may not know how to deal with."

Napanee watched his hands as she expected to hear he would never be with her again. She felt pins and needles in her cheeks, as if they were pressing against an abrasive surface. Her palms were cold, her ears hot. Her thermatic system was not doing what it was supposed to be doing. She found herself pressing on her toes, her heels raised. The leash of control she thought she had over him was stretching.

"I'm blind," Jeff said clearly.

She looked at his eyes reflexively. She felt someone had lifted her into the bucket of a hot air balloon which was about to take off into the wind across an expansive land of sharp mountaintops.

"I just heard you say you're blind. The way love is blind? Like poetry?"

"No, you heard me. I can see you this minute, but I have lapses when I can't see a thing. Maybe white shadows."

"You look fine to me, Jeff." Napanee was pacing with her arms folded across her chest. It was too obvious a way of expressing her outrage. It meant she did not want to leave, and yet was too impatient to stand for the way things were. She sat down again as if someone were coming to snatch it away.

"It comes and goes. The condition is degenerative. I've had it for a while."

"You've been to the doctors? Where is it going?"

"Either it will stay like this, or get better or I'll be totally blind."

Napanee blurted out in sudden anger.

"This is a brush-off. The worst brush-off I ever heard. You're blind like I'm deaf."

"I can't tell you anything else."

"I don't believe a word you said."

Napanee could only think of the end. She was furious.

"Why would I want you if you're really blind?"

She was so angry, she pushed against the table to move her chair backward. The coffee spilled over the rims of their cups. Without saying a word, or looking at Jeff, she strode out of the coffee shop and reached her car with no break in her pace. Her rage drove her to the nearest open boutique, where she had never before shopped. Napanee bought a green soft leather purse out of pure contempt for herself: she hated the colour and had nothing to go with it. By the time she got into the car again, she was calm, or at least she had grown cold. That is when she cried the tears of someone who had been taken, someone who had paid too much for something she did not want or need. The only comfort she had was the fact that no-one could see her, no-one could hear her, no-one would know the day after, and best of all, no-one would believe her if she told them what she was going through.

She wanted to be anything but herself. A large plastic garbage bag stuffed with out-of-style clothing destined for a thrift store would have been appropriate, as would have been the spare auto parts the garage mechanic shows he replaced. Anything incapable of remorse and anger, like a sack of flour left in the pantry so long it splits itself.

Rain fell timidly. Napanee wondered whether to make a dash for her car in the parking lot. Moist mall music dripped down on her. The moment had trapped her. The insignificance of it cried for a decision on action. Without that decision, time itself, naked time, kept her company, saying nothing, agreeing with everything, absorbing like a clear plastic shopping bag. Pushing open the door exposed her to the elements. Staying inside was like being at home on a boring day.

In the distance, she could see the Mortimer Ketchum Library, a building she had not visited for years because there was no reason to. Tufts of low-lying fog surrounded its foundations. A large white sign or banner hung on its upper floor: it was impossible to make out what was written on it.

Napanee carefully drove by the Library building and could clearly see it was closing: 'The Friends of the Library say Good-bye. For Sale'.

She was stunned, as she would have been stunned by the sudden drop in price of an article she had bought an hour before. Many thoughts raced through her mind: 'For Sale' meant the building was no longer an institution: it had now proclaimed it was a product. It was asking to join the ranks of tea biscuits, specialty pet food and boating accessories. Whether the building was momentarily within reach did not matter. If it had a price tag, it had a willingness to be treated as any other commodity. There was no loss of esteem or mobility in agreeing to enter the marketplace. Napanee could see it as an admission by the most celebrated race horse that at the end of days, it had another vocation, mundane or not, and an appointment at the glue factory, or at a French restaurant on the steak menu.

The next day, she took her Price to visit the Library.
"I want you to see something special. A place full of books."
"Mom, I know what a library looks like."
The Library was open for another month. Endowment money had finally run out and no one was prepared to pay hundreds of dollars instead of five for the cost of membership. The front desk had long ago stopped buying new releases. The books were not being properly restacked and the general reading area had the cramped look and smell of a second-hand bookstore. Instead of being generous with donations, members dropped off old magazines and discarded beach-read paperbacks which sat in piles in cardboard crates along the walls.

The carpeted bathtub was still there, almost buried under ring binders, bulletins, coverless books, staplers and scrapbooks. The nearby wall was covered with severely yellowed newspaper clippings about the book bin baby, complete with pictures of a toddler hanging over the rim of the bathtub.

"Why did you bring me here?"

"That's you in the pictures, Price."

Price could not make out any of the faces.

"How do you know that's me?"

"This is where you were born," she said clapping her hands together.

"In the bathtub?"

"That's right. You had so many friends here, I hated to take you home."

Price started reading aloud one of the articles. The mustiness of the place infiltrated his ability to understand where he was. The walls were old faces he barely recognized. The odours of thousands of books, hands, yells and silent breathings deepened the scent of well-hidden mould. Either this was an embrace, or a trap with lethal consequences. Price had no one to ask. The collar button on his shirt he was pulling at came off in his hand, dropping to the floor. He did not want to bend to retrieve it.

"Take me home.... »

Napanee could not understand Price's reaction. He was unresponsive in the car. When she got home, she called her father to say she would put in an offer to buy the Library.

That offer was a standard form legal document accompanied by a letter written on scented hand-made paper. Flecks of petals of buttercup, thyme and lily were noticeable at the rims of the sheet. Written in fountain pen, the letter expressed Napanee's great sadness in seeing the building suffer the fate it was experiencing, and her sense of responsibility in dealing with it as a local, honoured treasure. Some literature lives on, she wrote, while other books die. Bravo to all of the volunteers who kept the library alive, and seeing to it that its influence survives in the hearts of those who used it. She blotted the "o" in bravo to convey a fallen tear.

Eight months later, the Library committee accepted her offer, which it characterized with chagrin as the lowest and cheapest they had received, yet the only one which pledged not to tear down the building for at least seven years. In an unusual display of honesty, the committee insisted that one of the annexes to the legal document of sale contain a statement of principles. Buried in a score of resolutions and guarantees appeared a statement that none of the members wished to be known in the world of reading as people who voluntarily closed down a library. It said they were driven to the sad conclusion that while this specific repository of books would no longer be, its spirit and the spirit of every literate individual would settle on another institution. 'Let the world not think of us as Philistines', the maudlin annex cried out. It was signed by all the committee members except Mrs. Gordon who had spent a lifetime trying to convince people that the Philistines were just as literate as the ancient Romans, and that a slur on one meant a slur on the other.

"Close the stupid library. It doesn't seem to have done you any good."

"We are not going out on a sour note, Mrs. Gordon," the chairman said.

"Because of you, the computer is going to replace the book."

The psychologist prescribed home schooling as the best way to deliver Price's education. What she was saying was clear, almost maliciously uncompromising. It was a scold backed by a taunt designed to have him look at her and readily agree. She told Gerald that he was not ready to accept what a school environment had to offer. There was a right fit, and a wrong fit.

"He's very bright," she said, meaning that there was no other school in the area prepared to take Price as a student. "If you want my frank opinion, there has to be more input by his parents or parent. The fact that you're talking to me shows us what's really wrong. He's angry at his mother."

Gerald replied: "What do you mean he's angry at his mother. I'm angry at his mother. I'm angry at my wife. I'm not supposed to be angry at you, but I am."

Gerald refurnished a room to make it look as stark as a classroom. The TV set was removed, a group of simple desks, chairs and bookcases installed. He was unable to find a large, wood-mounted blackboard on a swing-stand. Gerald installed a series of blackboards, each the size of a desk top. A computer unit was placed near the window. Once it was all arranged, he sat on one of the unpadded chairs thinking he could probably teach Price himself. He had the school curriculum, some free time and what he thought was an ability to motivate. He shared the idea with Price, who could not look more disinterested. Even the suggestion that they try out the experiment brought Price to say: "I don't want to."

The tutors Gerald interviewed were young, shy, inarticulate, or the opposite. They were nothing like he had imagined: bespeckled older men in worn brown suits like his high school chemistry teacher, or heavy-set faded angry women like his home-room elementary school teacher. With amazement and discovery, he saw the transition of pedagogy shift generations, unsure the new face of education was capable of carrying on.

Gerald soon gave up and called a tutoring service to supply whoever was necessary.

Of the three tutors Gerald hired, Chazy had rare patience and humour. In fact, she had declared her rules the first time they met for a class in his kitchen. Chazy extended her hand, her fingers spread wide. Price smirked quickly and shook it.

"I'm eighteen. You're fourteen. I know more stuff than you do. I want to be an architect. You don't know what you want to learn. But you're a person. I'm a person. Let's respect that. Besides, my father is your dentist and your grandfather's."

Price would test her in obvious ways, then in more subtle ways. For the next two lessons, he came down to the study room ten minutes late, eating from a bag of chips or plate of French fries. On each occasion, she asked him to get her something to eat as well. When she had finished eating, he noted they only had half an hour left. Chazy asked for something more substantial to eat, with a diet drink. She had him running back and forth from the kitchen until their time was up.

"Hey, I didn't learn anything, Chazy."

He turned his pockets inside out to show he had nothing.

"You ate, so I ate." Chazy said, patting her belly.

There was a repeat performance the next time. Halfway through their hour, he told her he was not her waiter; and that she was hired to teach him math. Playing with her hair, she looked beyond him toward the kitchen.

"You sure you wouldn't want to eat more, Price?"

Two weeks later, he told her the homework questions she had given him were too easy. All his solutions were wrong. Chazy smiled as she crossed off each of his answers.

He drummed his pen on the desk to annoy her. In response, she began her own rapping.

"Do you have a separate sheet with the right answers?"

Price pulled out a sheet of paper from the back of his work book, asking what it was worth to her.

At their fourth meeting, she brought him a series of programming software. He was curious. Even more, he marvelled at the way she unpacked and displayed the floppy disks and the manuals. She was like a street vendor arriving ahead of her customers, unfolding and erecting an elaborate stand to hawk her wares. She stopped short of doing it all.

"You upload whatever you want. I brought it so you can take charge. Make all the mistakes you want."

"Incredible."

"Play with the software. I see you have a machine that can handle it. We can learn math through programming. That way, you'll be twice as smart when we finish."

Once he warmed to her, he was more comfortable with the structure she was imposing. Her concept of learning was not utilitarian, something he was not used to. His abiding assumption was that there was a goal to every gesture or even thought. His disbelief or scepticism heightened when she told him mathematics has a moral base: two numbers equate to a third because of a moral universe. If there were simply chaos, numbers would reflect disorder. When she made a point, her lips would form a pouting circle, mimicking a bad whistler. Numbers are good people, she would sometimes say.

"Why are they good people?" Price would ask on cue.

"Because they are good to each other. They rely on other numbers and they accommodate them out of respect," she said, looking as if she were blowing on hot soup.

"Have you ever poked a stick in water to see how deep it was? That's what praying is: poking inside yourself to see where bottom is."

"Are you a missionary?"

"I really don't know what you're talking about, Chazy."

"When I was nine years old, I wanted something my parents didn't want to buy, probably another doll. I prayed at my bedside so intensely for it, my room began to fill up with the scent of lilies and lilacs and trees in autumn. When my mother suddenly came into my room, she asked if I was burning incense. She called my father in, who thought there might be an electrical fire in the walls. My brother ran around the perimeter of the house to see if any of the neighbourhood kids were burning something in the bushes. Well, nothing was burning. There were no flowers or trees in my room. Just the scent of those intense plants that wafts up from your deep secrets."

Price figured she was leading up to a prank. Popping a gum ball in his mouth, he said, "What are you telling me, that I could fill a room with old baseball sweater perfume if I concentrated?"

Price noticed Chazy always seemed to have showered an hour before. Her hair was pulled back in a comb or elastic band behind her head. She gave the impression of an athlete fresh from a diving competition, quietly enjoying the glow of her performance.

The questions he asked had answers. It was the first time he could debate with someone who had more than a material sense. For example, she could not accept his view that order and cleanliness were, by definition, good. She did agree that what was good for Wall Street was good for Wall Street. The ability to buy another television set did not promote the ability to acquire another friend or send another message of gratitude.

Any similarity between Chazy and Napanee was mistaken. Before meeting Chazy, Price was under the impression all females were the same; similar in the way all dollar bills, or coins, or leaves or sandwiches, regardless of denomination were alike. Individuality was in the name, not the texture or essence. They were strict, single-minded, abrupt, self-contained and impatient, like cats.

"You like guys, Chazy?"

"Love them."

"How much?"

"As much as I want to?"

"Are you living with a guy?"

"A great guy. He's my father."

"When are you moving out?"

"Just because you want to doesn't mean I want to."

He had never had a sustained conversation with a girl or woman that did not involve the attribution or denial of blame. He had never spoken to a relaxed female, one who was not in a hurry to make a point and leave. Price could feel Chazy was concerned about him, which is why he childishly challenged her, and which is why he looked forward to each session, to see her again. Chazy could see over the months that he was becoming more obedient, more attentive, more dependent, maybe even obsessed with her. In order to bring him back to a manageable state, she told him one day:

"I have Dutch Elm disease. Price, I'm confiding in you."

He didn't know what to say except, "Isn't that for trees?"

"Most people think that. The vessels around my heart are turning into something like wood. I might have to stop tutoring, which I don't want to do. If they don't cure me, I could become as old as your mother in a few months. Do you understand what I'm telling you?"

Price told her she must be joking. Chazy said he was making such good progress, they could easily reduce the frequency of their sessions.

Price had Chazy drive him to the Library Building one pre-rush hour morning. In most abandoned buildings, shuttering the windows rarely prevents vandals from breaking the panes. Remarkably, all of the panes in both storeys were intact, maybe due to the location of the property. It was now on a fairly large traffic island bordered on one side by a service road leading to the largest shopping mall in the area. Perhaps it was the respect the community of shoppers still held for Mortimer Ketchum after whom the road and mall were named.

"You can't get in, Price."

"I don't want to get in. I wanted you to see it."

"What do I see?"

"That's me. That building is me. Can you believe my mother?"

"Here's the deal, Price. You will not get me to take sides against your mother. She has a way of loving you that is unique to her. She gave you a home. Make it your home."

"I have a home and nobody's there I can talk to."

"Then you're already better off than ninety-nine percent of the people in the world. Chazy had not seen him this agitated for a long time. She had no idea why he was acting out at this stage, except a recurrence of deep fear or manipulation. There was nothing she could add and little to do except to push his studies.

Algorithms replaced food and sports, yet were compatible with his home schooling. For two years, Price exhausted the 386, then the 486, tried parallel computing and then hit on the way to connect to the world-wide web using an accelerated dialing system. Although the military and the academic world seemed to have monopolized access to the web, Price's software in combination with a powerful computer competed more than favorably with private access codes coming on to the market.

He was fascinated by what he called sprouts. Having reached the end of a function, he saw it sprout into three or four different avenues, each with its own divergences once explored to the end. When he had trouble calculating because he had not yet perfected the particular math skill, Chazy was able to bring him through the difficulty once she unscrambled the logic he had used. Her solutions were usually in the nature of a short-cut, rather than a direct resolution of his statement. She confessed it was more an exercize in cheating, while Price found her approach a smart way to get to the solution faster.

Chazy checked on his progress once a week. Whenever he would arrive at a new platform, he would try reaching her at home, begging out of excitement in his message that she come over right away to see the results. She resisted taking his calls, thinking it best to have him explore on his own. She made much of his progress at each session, exaggerating her facial expressions and her tone of voice, as if she were doting on an infant. It delighted him that she was genuine, and thought the attention he was eliciting was deserved.

And so he was stunned that his increasing mastery of programming caused her several times to insist he did not need her anymore. That was not what he had imagined. He was being good, yet his reward turned into a withdrawal of her interest. Each time Price said plaintively he needed her to watch that he was still on the right track.

Gerald was so concerned about Price's intense involvement at the computer, he took him out to a rifle range on slow evenings. Each time they went, Price found the clientele consisted of obese or heavy men, most with crew cuts. A few were scrawny, if not under-nourished. He could not see how he fit in with this group until Gerald told him many of the people were policemen, sport hunters, accountants and collection agents. Unlike at a bowling alley, the rules here were strictly enforced. No alcohol, no private guns, time was up when time was up. Price quickly learned how to balance, grip and shoot the weapon, at first at the expense of hitting the target. His eye-hand co-ordination had benefited from his daily finger on the mouse. The major difference was the discharge of the bullet: raw, abrupt and simple-minded in its mission. He marvelled at his own physical engagement in the process of firing and reacting. He appreciated his grand-father's fretting over aim, but asked him to stop saying "Shoot to kill".

"It's just a target," Price said.

"I know, I know. You can pretend it is whatever you want it to be."

"I want it to be a hand made out of electrons that catches what I'm shooting."

"Okay, it's electrons."

"I'm pitching, it's catching. And we all get along."

Although he had only used computers for data storage, Gerald immediately saw the investment potential of what his grandson had created. Gerald called on two of investment bankers he knew, both of whom referred him to a major one, who could understand what he was trying to market. He soon met with a due diligence group and worked on a business plan. A syndicate was formed, an underwriter enlisted and a magnificent sale executed.

The Journal called the sale price of the software, bugs and all, "...excessive and a sign of things to come." Gerald's lawyer had structured the deal so that no-one knew the software C-In C-Out was created by a seventeen-year old. When Harry saw the article, he could never have guessed his role in stimulating the development of the Internet. All he could think of was borne out of jealousy. Why had he not thought of a way to sell pure air to the financial community?

There was so much money put away for Price in a foundation, Gerald considered it honest enough to take a little as his finder's fee to buy a farm replete with a standing crop of corn, a barn full of hay, farm vehicles and four sick cows. They all died in the pasture by the time he took possession. Using the tractor for the first time, he tied a chain around the necks of the upside down carcasses and pulled them away to a pit to be burned.

Price asked that twenty-thousand dollars be donated to the correctional facility he had attended, on the condition that the old guards wear buttons that read "Speed Counts". He also insisted that a more than fair compensation be given his math tutor Chazy who received her degree the day after the software deal had closed. Price went to the graduation exercises at the University hall partly out of appreciation.

Chapter 9

Price The Undergrad

Price's T-shirt bore the classic picture of Che Guevara, but with the word "Criminal" printed in red across the face. His professor told Price in open class to stop interrupting the lecture. The students had been waiting for a blow-up.

"If you don't like my approach to the subject, you're free to take any other history course you want."

Price was not going to move.

"The subject is Renaissance Politics. Why do you keep referring to American Imperialism in a Renaissance Politics class? Since class started half an hour ago, you've said American Imperialism four times. Since the course started, that's all you've talked about."

"Do you have a problem with the way I teach?"

"Do you have a problem with stuffing your political agenda so we can learn what went on in Italy six hundred years ago?"

One student stood up and complained he didn't pay tuition to watch a fight in a lecture hall. Another made a woofing sound as if he were a soccer vandal.

"Go complain to the Dean. Class is over."

"Professor, you're over."

Students threw their notes up in the air.

Price's club was the only conservative student group on campus. It had ten members and no budget because the student union refused to give it official status. The monthly speaker's forum featured graduate students before a very thin audience practicing the defense of their theses on the constitution, leadership roles and economic support systems.

No one took the club seriously. Even the few members and line-up of speakers faded after the first semester.

All of a sudden, it became notorious and therefore popular. Price paid for full page ads running on consecutive days in two student newspapers denouncing the "open" marriage of Simone de Beauvoir and Jean-Paul Sartre as a fraud, and both of them as "net exporters of trivia". A series of irate letters to the editors from staff and students depicting Price as a parochial sewage pit among other slurs prompted him to place more ads, this time naming individual professors he thought were feeding students "leftist thoughts even on the weather" under the guise of university learning. The named professors sent the newspapers a lengthy response co-signed by twenty others who asserted their right to academic freedom, and demanded Price be shut out of campus.

Since the club had no formal office on campus, someone went to the trouble of finding his apartment off campus and spraying graffiti on his door. He resumed the monthly speakers' forum and found the first session was packed with hecklers who came equipped with whistles, boom-boxes and bongo drums to drown out the speaker.

One of the fraternities was responsible for hiring three strippers who Price found in his apartment one night. Price reacted by shouting and throwing books at them to get them to leave. His efforts were photographed and pictures appeared in all the campus papers the next day, captioned "Price DeMann at the Speakers' Forum" or "Conservative Club Off-Hours".

He placed one more ad, this time announcing his candidacy for presidency of the student association. His platform, which was never accepted by the voting public, was based on the question, "What do warm beer, feminists and leftists have in common?"

Chapter 10

Dutch Elm Disease

Harry made a play for Chazy over a discussion on real estate. It was not intentional; and it looked like she was asking for it. Their encounter happened casually. She seemed relaxed, pliable, impressed by him, and this before she had said one word. She wanted something from him. If she was desperate, he would find the words to ease her desperation. He was so satisfied with the way he was going to handle himself, he began to script his day-dream the minute he saw her. Age was not going to be a factor. His cologne, too masculine for words, assured him easy passage.

Gerald hired Chazy to work for Price's foundation the same year Price went away to university. The foundation was investing in commercial properties. Chazy was a junior architect who had started managing her own father's portfolio. Since she was making little progress in the professional firm she had joined, it was an easy decision to leave, even though news of her departure stimulated a sudden move by the partners to pay her more to stay.

She said many times she chose architecture as a profession because her father was a dentist.

"After you pull your patient's teeth, why don't you bury them or crush them?"

Her father thought her naive. "Some of these teeth are claws. Each has a personality. I only keep the remarkable ones. There is at least one canine for each year of my practice. It gives me a sense of perspective when I look back at my collection."

Chazy took a real estate course, and quickly learned the nature of the market and basic appraisal techniques. Gerald was interested in long-term investment and development, and told her many times he was not interested in flips. He gave her the latitude to create a blended investment strategy. She was buoyed by the trust placed in her.

Chazy made an offer to buy on a group of row houses on a block rezoned commercial. The plan was to keep the brownstone façades of the houses and reconstruct the rest of the property into a low-rise commercial centre. Harry owned the real estate and had no idea she worked for his son's foundation.

At their meeting, she wore a light-coloured business suit, a jeweled butterfly pinned to her lapel. She was twenty-four and retained her straight-backed athletic look. Harry was forty. The two grey hairs around his temples got plucked every time they appeared.

"I'll sell you the block only because you're asking. You have me under a spell," he told her over lunch.

"If you're so enamored with me, why sell it? Give it to me for free," she said, putting down her fork. His asking price was three times the municipal evaluation.

"You want the block so your people can build a hundred storey skyscraper on it. Who is your boss? Tell him that selling it is like giving it away," Harry said, pointing his finger. "When can we get down to our business?"

"I have two bosses. One is almost seventy years old and the other is nineteen. Neither of them could possibly appreciate your generosity."

Harry asked her to work for him at twice the salary. He needed a partner he could trust, someone tough and good-looking enough to manipulate tenants. He moved to touch the jewellery piece on her right lapel, appreciated her simple chain necklace, visible at her open collar. He sighed at her.

Although Harry thought he was exuding magic, Chazy tagged him as immature. The problem was that he had what she wanted, and she had yet to find a way to maneuver him into position. She was glad she had earlier refused to meet over lunch. From past experience, if lunch was necessary, it was a rushed affair at a fast-food restaurant of her choice. They met at a take-out burger place at her insistence. Harry was surprised at the venue. She ordered the greasiest items on the menu with a coffee and simply drank the coffee. Taking her cue, Harry ordered double fries with a drink and an extra large piece of cherry pie. Her purpose was to keep her colleague eating from his and then her tray as a bonding experience until his stomach could no longer tolerate the heavy oil.

"Mr. Souply. Can I call you Harry? You're a very stimulating guy. Up front. Likes to reach out for what he doesn't have. An optimist. A real Candide."

"Do I know Candide? And is that a compliment, Chazy? Can I call you Chazy? Since you're in the market, maybe you'd like to buy my own house. Want to come over and see it with me?" Harry suggested.

"You don't know what kind of girl I am, Harry."

"A very smart one with a very smart body."

As he said that, his belly began to rumble and knot. He reached for his iced drink which he finished with repeated draws on the straw. He was in distress for a moment until the feeling of nausea went away.

"Harry, can I confide in you? You don't want to get involved with me."

"Why wouldn't I? Are you married to a prize fighter?"

"No. Worse," she sighed as she looked down.

"What could be worse?"

"I have a wooden chest under this blouse."

Harry widened his eyes. He visualized a wooden toy stick man he had as a child. He peered at her neckline.

"Dutch Elm disease. Had it since I was a teenager. My women's things are turning into woody tissue. It's just disgusting to look at," she said, looking at his mouth widening.

"You're not... serious?" he asked carefully.

"I would show you but you're a guy who would want to touch. And that's not a good idea. You might get stuck with the same thing. You would blame me for waking up with it one morning. Then you wouldn't want to sell me your second-rate real estate."

"How can you tell you have the disease. I mean, how does it affect you?"

As soon as he said that, the pressure on his bowel came back with such force he had to run from the table.

Chazy knew trees were made of meat. Diseases rarely, if ever, jump from trees to humans. Chazy loved to chop wood, burn bark, whittle sticks and gather leaves. She did not eat meat. She fulfilled the innate hankering for meat by reveling in wood. Those who argue the need for meat is recent, at least post-diluvian, would hold that eating animals is an acquired taste or a social, not genetic norm. Similarly, if Chazy felt the need to climb an elm, it was a learnt desire. She liked to sand a small plate of mahogany, or peel strips of birch bark for use as paper. She often placed her cheek against the oak top of her mother's linen chest until it was warm. Chazy sharpened pencils by chewing away at the wood to expose more lead. Maybe she did pick up the disease from a sheet of plywood beneath her mattress or the cushion-less stool in her kitchen.

What she called Dutch Elm disease was sadness she felt for the substitution of wood by plastic, or the distance modern society created from the fruits of the forest. It was an unnatural distance that gave her spasms or cramps, especially when she was with men who sought to challenge her self-worth. The normal elasticity of her capillaries and the flexibility of her various valves gradually hardened under hydraulic pressure. It gave her pleasure to be that way, the way an elm or a pine tree girds itself in the face of danger, and even communicates distress to its standing neighbours.

Chazy looked distantly at the window.

"When you have the problem, you can't tell who is handsome or ugly. It obscures your judgment about people based on the way they look."

The row of houses was Harry's highest achievement to date. For a time after defrauding old people, he lent small amounts of money at high interest rates to borrowers who operated Ma-and-Pa grocery stores, or who repaired cars or furniture. Harry always told them this was not his money, that he himself had borrowed it from bad people, and that if it weren't returned on time with all the interest, they would have to answer to someone who would not listen to excuses. He even showed off a thin scar under his chin where he had nicked himself shaving. Sometimes he would demonstrate the irregular alignment of his smallest finger which he had broken by accidentally closing the car door on it.

"They first get mad. Then they go after you."

Many of his customers, after two years, owed him five thousand dollars on a two thousand dollar loan. To avoid a visit from terrible people, the borrowers offered their spouses and relatives as guarantors, or gave up family heirlooms as security. Harry took the row of houses as security for a two hundred thousand dollar loan to cover a gambling debt. The borrower gambled away the loan within a month, and thought crying in front of Harry would save his property. Harry wanted three million dollars for the block, either from the previous owner or from Chazy.

Harry told the owner quite frankly:

"You know what real estate goes for these days?"

"But I live here."

"You see it as a house. What a waste. You have to look at it as a development. Why were you wasting your time living in prime territory when the world was crying for a multi-unit up-scale project. Shame on you for slowing down everyone's plans."

"When can I get it back?"

"Probably never. You weren't born for high finance."

Harry soon came down in price for two reasons. Chazy told him she was not interested in him or his property. The foundation real estate lawyer found a title defect in the transfer of property to Harry which would require new signed documentation from the prior owner. Harry was not prepared to ask his borrower for any favours, especially since the borrower's wife laid a charge of criminal usury against him. To settle the entire mess, he convinced his borrower to become his partner in the real estate sale. Then he approached Chazy again. She offered to buy for one third the asking price, which Harry accepted on one condition. He wanted cash, not in the sense of payment at closing. He wanted a pile of dollars delivered to him at the signing, accompanied by a counting-of-the-bills ceremony. She did not oblige.

Chapter 11

Marriages

The tax advantage to Price of owning a tree farm was extraordinary. For some time, Chazy had been trying to book a helicopter trip over a forested tract within one hundred miles of the city to buy acreage. Gerald did not want to go at all. For some reason, Price wanted to wait.

The wait was over. Price asked Chazy to make arrangements although not in the area she had in mind. They would have to fly by commercial jet for an hour, and then take a helicopter to the site he had found.

"Is there a tax reason why we're going out of the area?" she asked at the airport.

Price said there was a better reason.

Once over the site, Price asked the helicopter pilot to land in a wide clearing. As they came closer to the ground, the pilot could see the grassy area seemed to be wet and boggy. He brought the helicopter up again and set down at a clearing on a very slight but solid slope.

As on most assignments, the pilot had little to do while waiting to take off. He learned after the first year of trips he could only rely on himself for constructive time. With little more than an hour, often unpredictably stretching to five, he devised the most suitable activity: knitting. The pilot created knitted pockets and hats for his throttles. His tool bag was a tight crochet. . His gloves had a fancy cuff. Today he felt like playing with gimp.

Price took Chazy's hand, leading her to the edge of the forest. Whatever the forest darkness held, it was not tainted with the sense of overwhelming loss felt in the city.

"The rules say you have to be in the business on a part-time basis to get a deduction. That means you have to be on the site at least twice a year... How do you know this place is for sale?" Chazy asked.

Price said he had received the particulars from an agent. He had even spoken with the mayor of the town at the foothill of the forest. He told Price to call him Hawkeye, and welcomed him to the community.

The tract of land was an elongated bubble of rock covered with woods, very much like the reverse side of a soup spoon. Deer, raccoons and grass snakes hid behind trunks and collapsed tree foliage on the forest floor. A stream of cold water flowed from an underground source mid-way up the eastern incline, eventually making its way to a lake near the populated area. A few natural clearings could be found, caused by spot lightning fires or erosion exposing gray bedrock. At the highest point, a ripple of distant blue-hazed hills spread into the horizon. Through the underbrush, a fox watched Price while a heron noticed the couple from the air.

"This is a stand of Dutch Elms, Chazy."

They were standing twenty feet from the nearest tree. He invited her to venture a bit into the grove. She refused to move, her arms folded in obstinacy.

"They're all healthy. The wood makes excellent specialty furniture. Did you bring a saw? I forgot mine," Price said.

"Why are we here? If I knew we were going hiking, I would have worn boots."

Price looked at her as if he were about to take a favorite book off the shelf. She still looked as fit as when he had first met her, ready to sprint if called to action or run through a series of cartwheels. Her khaki-colored skirt provided a matching background for the white and blue wild-flower petals waving at her knees.

"You're as strong, not as sick as any of these elms... I need you Chazy, but not as a teacher."

"As what, your mother?"

"Not my mother."

"I don't like younger men."

"You don't like men. But maybe there's a way you can like me."

Chazy was not comfortable with the discussion. She did not want to offend Price, or keep the pilot waiting, or walk into a grove of trees that might contract and make breathing difficult. She sensed this day, this moment had been coming for years, yet she never bothered to prepare a scripted dialogue. Chazy had only prepared "no" for an answer.

They were standing on the plateau of a mild hill. Chazy could see more substantial and jagged hills beyond the river in the valley. The sun's heat was dry. The insects were not bothersome.

"I like you, Price."

"The same way you like real estate. I think too much about you."

Chazy stopped him. She said she had her universe, he had his. His perception of the great map of things unfolding did not match her views. Cause and effect were morally related. Things were not moral simply because they always existed.

"Price, we're meant to be together if I and you decide it; not because it was decided for us or because we just happen to be here. And I deserve you only if you deserve me."

"If I told you we are in a sweep of history, and we're being carried off in the big sweep."

"Whoa! Such big words coming out of your mouth."

"Okay Chazy, I don't know how to say anything you won't look at as being too young."

"Price, I'm not making fun. Believe me. I'm just... trying to slow you down."

She was telling him she was afraid; it was something he could not understand as an impediment. They stood looking at each other. They did not approach the stand of trees. They imagined it. The pilot was at a crucial point in completing a gimp place mat. With an intricate five-colour peacock motif, the project was a first for him. He was planning to send it to his knitting teacher. He managed to effectively shout, "Five minutes to take-off" to Price, so that he could tie off the ends.

They married three months later, then left for the Amazon rain forest on their honeymoon.

They had sent Harry an invitation to the wedding a week after they were married. Chazy agreed the ceremony should be small and thought it appropriate that Price's father be one of the guests. Price had an open mind, but Napanee sided with her father. Gerald did not want to be near or see Harry. The only thing he would have told him was that he was not finished with him yet.

"The last time I thought about him, he did not have a name and he was not there." Gerald said.

"Who are you talking about?" his wife asked.

"Remember a long time ago, Napanee had a male friend who lived in our house for a few months and then left?"

"How long ago was that?"

"Very long ago."

"Well, how can I remember Napanee's friends that far back. I don't even know most of the people here today."

"It doesn't matter," Gerald reassured her.

The ceremony was graceful and meticulously timed. At Cheryl's urging, Napanee brought a clipboard and pen attached with a curled ribbon. As each scheduled event ran its allotted time, Napanee ticked off the corresponding box, and had Cheryl push forward the next in line, whether it was the band, the speeches or dessert. Her mother was too remote to be useful, except to comment on the dresses or mousse as they passed her by.

Many of the guests were Gerald's business associates, if not family. Price invited a group of software partners he had funded. Chazy brought a number of friends she had made and retained from her university days. Napanee really had no one special she wanted there except some people who worked for her. She sent a memo rather than an invitation to fourteen people in the office, specifying where and when they were expected. Fourteen made up two tables perfectly, and so she mentioned that consorts and special friends were not party to the event. Someone had copied the memo, pinned it to the bulletin board, and circled the word 'consort' with a remark in the margin "what's that?"

When Chazy had met Harry over the real estate transaction, she had no idea he was Price's father; nor did Harry realize for whom Chazy worked. She only understood Harry Souply's connection when she was going through Gerald's folders he had given her, one of which bore Harry's name. She found a number of early pictures of Harry, as well as several private detective reports.

Harry learned of the wedding while he was fishing with his girlfriend he called Felicia, who hated the outdoors. He was standing on the shore, watching a snake dart out of the bush, slither into the water, catch a curious fish nibbling near a rock, and swallow the fish whole once it came back to the shore. To him, the spectacle was novel, he thinking why it was he could not swallow living creatures whole.

His girlfriend saw the tail end of the incident and immediately screamed in fear and disgust. She ran to the car for safety, where she rolled up the windows and stayed inside, sobbing. When he came over to talk Felicia out of the car, she opened a window and threw whatever she could at him, including a flashlight, suntan lotion bottle and a section of the Sunday newspaper.

"Give me the keys. I'm going home!"

"We haven't caught any fish yet!" Harry protested.

"You didn't tell me there were man-eating snakes here."

Harry said it was the first time he saw a grass snake that large. Coming to recognize he would have to take her back to the city or else face unrelenting whining, he acquiesced with a slap of the hand on his own bottom. He took the time to pick up the newspaper she had thrown, glancing at a small item on the social page, headlined *Price weds Chazy*. The article summarized the essentials of the wedding, which Harry accepted as a matter of fact.

As he folded away the paper, the oddest feeling came over him. He was immobilized by a draining power at his feet, as if another great snake was in the process of consuming him whole. Blood receded from his face and neck: he was in freefall but not moving.

"Are you all right?" Felicia asked. "You look like you have flour on your face."

"That's not flour."

"What is it?"

"I'm turning into a corpse. A standing, stalking stiff."

"Why are you doing that? Do you have allergies?"

"I have corpse disease. People treat me like I'm dead. I don't believe it."

"Want some water or something?"

"To drown in."

Part of his life had just been lived for him, yet he had not been invited to the event. He was growing weak at the thought he had missed the only train in this century, and would have to wait until he was near death to catch the next one. Harry felt left out of a situation he had not created nor controlled. Numbness, disappointment, anger, all the emotions that mixed together when an unexpected bill arrives or a large bank balance is no longer there: they covered him like warm quicksand. Felicia thought he was taking his time to get back at her, until she noticed his forehead had lost its power to wrinkle, and his face lost its scheming flush.

As Harry shouted an obscenity at another driver from his car window, a deranged bee flew straight into his mouth. It caused a vibrating commotion on his upper palate and tongue, finally leaving in a drunken buzz before it could be swallowed. The bee gave him the idea to marry his girlfriend in order to test his son. Harry intended to invite Price to his wedding in the same way he had trapped the insect in his mouth.

Harry was very busy before his wedding date. He made a short list of girlfriends he had been intimate with in the previous few months. With super-human effort and patience, he took each out for supper at the same restaurant on consecutive nights. Four consecutive meals qualified him for free food on the last night. He proposed marriage to each girlfriend, most of whom laughed it off as a prank, even though he insisted on the seriousness of the enterprise. Yet they all jokingly said yes and whispered he was sweet, questioning his true intentions.

"We would make marriage history, Gwen," Harry hummed.

"Idiot weds idiot."

"Not that way. Think of our kids."

"I have a beautiful face and you have a great back of the head."

"Our picture would be on the society pages."

"Maybe on the police blotter. If my parents heard I was engaged to a bum like you, one of us would not survive until the wedding."

At the last meal, the previous night's girlfriend returned to the restaurant to retrieve her forgotten umbrella. When she saw him sharing onion soup with another candidate, she pulled the tablecloth from beneath their elbows, sending the table-ware and soup onto their laps and the floor. The two who remained enchanted with the proposal in marriage soon received a singing telegram which consisted of the *dum-dum-de-dum* of the Bridal March, and an invitation to the wedding of Harry and his current girlfriend, without a reply card. Before leaving, the messenger sang "Please don't bother coming" to the melody of *Take Me Out To The Ball Game.*

For Harry, women were not merely playthings. They were beach balls, squeezable in the heat of the day, full of bounce, light and disposable. Polygamy was less desirable than monogamy because of the terrible strain of accountability. Any institution that bound people together had no business existing, since the only reason one person wanted to be bound to another over an extended period of time was the aroma of her steak and potatoes, her money or her addictive availability. That's right, marriage was made for addicts. For the fly-by-nighters or the grazers and nomads, good relationships, as long as they lasted, were defined by the rule of impulse.

Since Harry said his girlfriend was extremely beautiful, the minister told him in advance he would be wearing a boxer's helmet and mouth guard. The minister had been punched at a number of ceremonies by the groom who thought his eyes were unnecessarily lingering over the bride. Those were the grooms who had told the minister their fiancées were very beautiful.

"You might think it strange. I have no insurance, and I already lost a tooth."

Harry promised not to touch him, that he was not a violent person. He could not change the minister's mind. The minister reminded him of his English high school teacher, a punctilious, easily upset gentleman who could not understand why students would not want to memorize sonnets. The minister and teacher had similar webs of veins in their cheeks, and rattled their hands like unwanted appendages to display disagreement.

"They say one thing and because everyone is nervous, their personalities change or something. I could do something else for a living."

"So what if your wife was there too, standing beside you?"

"You could punch her out. Why would I do that to her?"

Harry could not find another minister who lived in Felicia's area for the date he wanted.

"What if you wore sunglasses? I couldn't see what your eyes were doing if they were covered."

"You would imagine worse. You would break my ribs. Listen, the reason you told me your bride was extremely beautiful was not to brag, but to warn me," the minister chided.

"Not to brag. It's the truth. I'm very proud of the fact."

Felicia was taken by surprise by his drive to marry her. They had worked together well on a major scam, although when it flopped, she thought they were over. She accepted because she needed him to pay debts she could not cope with. She had even thought he proposed in order to scare her off, after he complained she didn't wash enough. He was ten years older than she was. Why was she here, she often asked herself. Mainly because she was no good as a forensic accountant: she had no idea what that a mismatched sum on an invoice and a bank draft meant there was something fishy going on. Maybe it was just an error, she would conclude. People always make mistakes. She was too reticent to think dishonesty was a reason for mathematical incongruity. Nothing matched, ever. Why should double billing and single payment be a signal?

However, she was honored at the marriage proposal because she thought little of herself. She emoted too easily and readily confessed she was not worthy of any sustained attention. Smart enough at work to file documents in the right folders, she had no need to prove herself any further. Felicia took Harry seriously, so much so she bought a book on meditation at the all-night pharmacy. It was a way to begin the edification of her inner self so it could become a wife. This was after the fact: she thought the title of the book was Medication when she paid for it at the check-out.

She told the clerk the next day the book was being returned.

"It has dog-ears," the clerk said.

"What's that?"

"The cover and some pages are bent. Did you read this and now you want to return it?"

"I started to until I realized it was the wrong title."

"Well, this is a pharmacy. We can't resell it now that it's used."

"But my fingers were clean when I touched it."

Unlike many men she had known, Harry liked to read. He was always reading street signs and instructions on cans and menus. He loved to cut out articles from the sports section of the newspapers, which he inserted between the pages of current men's magazines he kept in disarray around his night-table. He spent time reading things on his computer screen, often asking her if she needed anything to read. Literacy for her was a value greater than good looks in a man: it meant depth, and depth meant the ability to be honest, interesting and maybe loyal.

Price did not respond to Harry's wedding invitation. Not a call or e-mail. Harry checked the mail, his computer. He was not going to call. He paced, he lost sleep, he broke pencil tips and snapped toothpicks in his mouth. He glared at things, glared at Felicia, and watched TV without being absorbed in sitcoms. No response, absolute silence which he took as a loud message of denial. Harry went to the zoo alone to look at the monkeys. Chimp fathers were playing with their chimp sons in the cage. Harry could see they were playing to the crowd. Who knew whose monkey was whose son? He spat into a tissue because of the smell. After the ceremony, Harry thought he had gotten married for nothing.

He did have major reservations about his wife. She pro-duced so much saliva he thought, he had to spit after each kiss. She told him he was exaggerating and that spitting during intimacy was a disgusting thing to do. Just to please him, be-cause he was such an energetic and therefore interesting person to her, she tamped her tongue with a little sponge which she then bit into. Harry complained those spongettes lying about on the dresser, night table and floor, reminded him of unclean underwear that belonged in a hamper.

To further drive home his point during the honeymoon, Harry refused to drink from the same cup she had used, or share an apple or straw, or even a baseball cap that may have had the slightest atom of perspiration in its band. If her palm was moist immediately after a shower, Harry could not bring himself to hold her hand. Very soon, all her secretions overwhelmed him. He abandoned her on the eighth day of their marriage, while she slept in a second bed at the Shore Line Hotel at Virginia Beach. He left her some cash, an almost maxed-out credit card and a "Goodbye" written in her lipstick on a little sponge.

Harry's sense of self-worth was based on his respect for obligation. He was responsible when no one stepped forward to assume that responsibility. The weight of being counted on was too heavy to bear many times, actually all of the time when it irritated or pressed or pushed him into doing what he did not want to do. If there were a choice between helping the world and helping himself, of course he would favour the world if it did not interfere with an appointment or the middle of breakfast.

When she awoke, she thought it strange that Harry was not in the room. She felt around the bed to discover she had been sleeping on her meditation book. The only crumpled page was the one where Step Three began, where the secrets of meeting your own soul in the locker room were simply and briefly laid out.

Chapter 12

Price Meets People

Chazy thought it best to find Price an office away from the Foundation. Many of the calls he was receiving came from software creators looking for financing or more contacts. She found him a sublet for eight months in lower Manhattan where most of the callers were centered. His office was furnished, consisted of three rooms, reception area and a boardroom. Since he was on a lower floor of the World Trade Center facing south, the view from his windows was obscured.

Price at first saw anyone who called. All were young, some accompanied by a consultant, or a lawyer or an accountant. All had a business plan of sorts, most waved their hands out of creative enthusiasm when describing how their product would do away with computer keyboards, or traditional telephones or bulky hard drives. They made extraordinary faces and race car noises when detailing the ramp-up in speed or the shrinkage of size or the enormity of capacity. Those who leaned over his conference table to underline passages in his copy of the business plan book, he quickly dismissed. Those who were rude, or ungraceful, or shy, or twitchy, he let speak without interruption. Others benefited from an observation or a request to repeat something that earlier had been glossed over. Many forgot their pens or cell-phones when they left. One entrepreneur gave him a miniature wind-up toy. A large minority knocked over glasses of water. A three-man team made squeaking noises as they nervously swiveled in their chairs. The procession of dot.com faces coo-ed to Price as if to a baby, entertaining, making lively gestures, bringing rapture to an open mind.

Napanee was no exception. She came punctually with Cheryl. Napanee had no problem asking her son for money. Price insisted she come to his office to discuss business. Aside from the inconvenience of going to Manhattan, it did not strike her as discordant that a mother would try to convince a child, no matter how mature, to invest in her activity. It was purely business: she was capable of risk management; the product and services were time-tested.

Although Cheryl strongly urged her to bring him gourmet cookies, Napanee only brought with her extra copies of her business plan.

"I've never given him cookies before. I'm not going to start now."

She was proficient in her work. Cheryl was one of her two managers. She had forty commission agents, four web-sites and one hard-copy newsletter sent to fifteen thousand subscribers. She had gone beyond product-testing. Her group of companies performed product imaging, focus group analysis and litigation support. She had also bought a bakery specializing in mail-order heavy sugar pies with optional diet syrup in an accessory plastic pack.

"Of course you can say no, Price."

"My only question is whether your business is too diffuse."

"Am I all over the place?"

"Why do you need the bakery?"

In her defense, Napanee said all the activities were making money.

"So why do you need another three million?" Price asked.

"Because if I don't pay you back you have the right never to speak to me again."

"We know that's what will happen. Do you want to risk it?"

"There is no risk."

Price saw she lacked the nervous edge of the other candidates for funds, yet she was deferential. He was pleasantly surprised to find himself judging his mother. She was a much better presenter than most applicants. Napanee never lost focus, had a ready response and was dressed one notch above the standard called for. She sounded knowledgeable and willing to learn more with venture money.

"Find another financing partner and I'll talk to him."

"That doesn't help me Price."

"Are you afraid to use your own money?"

Napanee waited, licking the beginning of the words she was about to express.

"The only way I can raise my own money is by knocking down the Library, and selling the land."

"The Library?"

"The Library."

"Do what you have to."

"I take that to mean you'll think about it."

Napanee had patience with Price because she could predict her son would fall into line. Her maternal pull gave her the advantage she could predict. Her words resonated in him in a way the words of any other person could. What may have seemed to be business between them was a mere testing of the family bond. Price owed a debt of creation to her. It was a totally unpayable and unforgivable debt he could not negotiate.

She wrote him a note which she tore up. Her articulation was magnificent. Children need their mother, not the other way around. She could understand those horrible famine stories of mothers eating their babies. It was an act of last resort, yet it was natural. A tree can consume its own fruit because it is the bearer. The producer has a right to eat his product. And what is the obligation of the child? Self-sacrifice for the mother's will. What was wrong with Price? What was his problem?

Looking over her shoulder, Price noticed she had in front of her an open book of statistics, probably a government report. The pages were heavily underlined and she was in the process of highlighting in water-colour green a column at the bottom. If that did not irritate him enough, Price was startled by what she then did. With her left hand, she nervously burrowed into the underlying pages until she grasped the top corner of a random page and ripped it off in an uneven strip. Crunching it into a ball, she put it into her mouth, chewing it like a wad of gum. Her jaws ground the paper, no doubt shredding, tenderizing and watering it. After swallowing, she repeated the process, this time pulling the strip all the way down the left margin of the page. A glossy dot of black appeared at the left corner of her lips.

After a few weeks, Chazy called early in the morning to see if he had enough. She said she did not want to emote on the phone. Her message, though, was that she thought it best that they were together. Price could not understand what she was asking. He had not seen such a variegated flow and show for years.

"This is how business should be, Chazy. Out of the dozens of ideas I looked at, maybe there were two or three that were solid. What's more important is seeing all this activity and brain power in such a concentrated way. I love it. A real parade. Why don't you come here for a while."

"Why, Price, are we a couple?"

"I'm afraid to say it. We should be."

Silence intervened. The last thing she wanted to convey was a whine. Plainly, she did not like being apart from Price. She worried about him and hated being alone now that he was in her life. She always thought that being married would bring her more confidence rather than less. Her source of strength began to emanate from his and not from within.

"Any projects you want to invest in?"

"The one I'm seeing in an hour. The wiz-kid must be eighteen at most. His team mates are just out of high school. I saw them last week and told them to come again."

"When are you flying back?"

"Soon… I have a problem with my mother. She asked for money, and is threatening to tear down the Library as a way of getting financing out of me."

"That's not good, Price. It's a part of you. It used to be a part of you."

"Why don't you see about putting in an offer. An anonymous offer, with the building intact. Not too high. See if she bites."

Chazy had little to do with Napanee over the years. They were certainly on quick speaking terms; neither had extended patience for the other. Chazy would tell Price she felt she was not happy having made no closer ties with his mother.

They had nothing at length to say that would have been of interest to the other. Napanee could have talked up Chazy's outfits, although there was no point. They were not friends.

They could not do things together because Chazy was drawn to museums while Napanee preferred a good trade show or a grand opening. There was so much effort required to make something up, their relationship could not even support five minutes together at a café.

"Do you know your mother has never read a work of literature, and that I have never read a store catalogue cover to cover?"

What she did not dare tell him was that Napanee was essentially selfish, superficial and disconnected from reality. She did not feel it was right to unload her distaste or unease. There was nothing he could do about her, except to keep her influence on him at bay. If there was any influence, it had already infiltrated. Mother-and-daughter-in-law jokes were not the stuff she wanted to validate. Chazy wished she would not be hurtful or use her position to corrupt their marriage.

On his brief walk to the office, he saw something unusual: a cat without a collar slowly making his way along the sidewalk, as if it were walking against a forceful wind. It was chewing on one side of its mouth. At first, it looked like a piece of gristle, the end sticking out near his molars. As it got closer, Price could see the object was a baby's rubber nipple, and that the cat was sucking, not chewing on it. The round head and ring of the nipple entered and exited its lips as its mouth worked. There was no sign it had swallowed a baby or anything else. It looked content to play with the squishy object as it sauntered.

Price was then approached by a man who had striking long sideburns, was well-shaven, wearing an expensive cologne that was subtle enough to be mistaken for the fresh scent of new clothes. He had a circular birthmark below one sideburn, which made it look like an exclamation mark. Price did not know whether to contain or exhibit his outrage when asked in a drawl for a thousand bucks.

"Where's your weapon?"

The mugger tilted his head as if he were a taunted animal denied the meat under his nose. He attacked, hitting Price across the side of his face with a heavy wrench, grunting: "The money, the money."

Price had never been struck in the face, or any part of his body, by anyone. He almost fell backward, thinking how exposed he had allowed himself to be. Intertwined with his pain, self-reproach welled up. In his dizziness, he moved slowly for his wallet. He could not understand why the stranger had decided to relate to him as he had. Price dropped his hand from his face, and aimed a kick at the mugger's left leg. He missed. Another blow to the head, which sent Price to the pavement. His elbow was grazed; no bones though were broken.

Price must have sat on the Wall Street curb in a daze for at least five minutes. The siren of a police car yelped, the ground shook. A grinding explosion reverberated in broad daylight. His head pulsed, but the street stopped. A few blocks down, many floors up, airplanes struck buildings and a billow of smoke, plaster, insulation and glass splinters was about to wash the pavement and fog over the morning.

Someone lifted him by the armpits, dragged him a few yards, then helped him hobble two blocks until he rested again on a curb. Singed pieces of aluminium paper and wallboard were falling out of a dense cloud. The pedestrians were running toward the pierce of fire sirens as if in anticipation of a parade. The pain and commotion in his head were being acted out in the office lobbies and café entrances before him.

For days after the Twin Towers collapsed, Price scanned casualty lists to see if his wiz-kid had been killed or survived.

He had no way of communicating with him because all the papers were in the office.

When he thought about the collapse, he kept visualizing the Library collapsing. He thought increasingly about it, wanting to get on a plane to visit the site, to make sure it was safe. He did not need stitches over the wounds in his scalp and his left cheekbone. That was his own diagnosis. Getting immediate medical attention was out of the question. He managed with the first aid basket he kept at home.

Price had to move out of his apartment because of the particles in the air. He did not want to leave the city. Lower Manhattan smelled of burnt cement and ceiling tiles. He had seen the buildings go down; he had watched the images on television so many times. He struck up easy conversations with policemen and soldiers in the area. Everyone had a story of near-death and death, and a photo. The reason the mugger had attacked him was to save his life. The city had saved him through the brusque hand of a stranger who probably knew danger and could sense the impending death of thousands. A *deus ex machina* uncluttered, driven by personal greed and self-gratification, was an active prophet seeking someone else's welfare, wearing an exclamation on his face.

Within days, questions about the motivations of the terrorists surfaced. What drove them to kill themselves and others? Didn't America's wealth and oppression of nations foment terrorism? Who was the real victim? When Price first heard them, he absorbed them as sick satire. As they proliferated, he felt under attack a second time. He wrote a brutal response to what he called the "left-wing gone suicidal". No media outlet published it except for the Herald, which reduced the two thousand word essay to a five line letter to the editor. Writing the essay solidified his theories of the enemy within and the slide to self-destruction caused by loose language and loose loyalties. He could no longer take for granted that strangers in his own land shared his values or that cultural differences did not matter when it came to the striving for a common standard of living. He wrote:

"It saddens me to admit people are not what they seem. This is no more reliable than the man in the street. The man is gone. The street is gone."

The fact was that what made him happy or comfortable did not necessarily have the same effect on others. He was so incensed he could only bond with policemen and firemen. He felt more comfortable with his mugger, who had an apolitical agenda which did not compromise his patriotism. The mere fact Price was victimized on Wall Street demonstrated the capitalist enterprise continued to attract advantage-seekers whose aim was not to destroy. The cat he had seen chewing on a nipple was the attacker's precursor. It was not conscious of where it was, what it was doing. It had the feline prerogative of ignoring whatever was of no interest, and insisting on its own way of life.

Many lists appeared in the papers and on the barricades at Ground Zero. After two weeks, Price spotted the name of the wiz-kid under "S" in a posted government list. It appeared just above "Souply, Harry". The tender spot on Price's cheek that had borne the attack, throbbed for a while, then scarred. The throbbing reassured him he was alive.

These were lists of death. No-one wanted to read them. Everyone did. Why didn't they post lists of the living? The pictures of missing relatives taped to poles, walls and impromptu shrines were flags of despair. The pictures were invariably over-exposed, too tiny or too formal to permit a good understanding of why they were there and not in a photo album in a private living room. The lists were clear, maybe ambiguous because of a few spelling mistakes. They were very public.

Gerald looked after the financing commitments Price had made. His priority, though, was to find Harry. He knew he could not be dead, and probably had not been anywhere near the Trade Center in September, or before, for that matter. If Harry was not pulling a crude scam, Gerald would at least consider his death an interesting, if not welcome, development.

Someone called Felicia Souply was among the first to apply for widow's benefits which would have amounted to about eight hundred thousand dollars. Gerald found that intriguing given that she was listed as a common law spouse.

Her story was simple. Harry left in the morning for a meeting on the ninety-first floor and called her at eight-thirty as he was entering the building. No, he didn't work there, and yes, he had been there before. He was not a client, so he would not appear in the client database. Harry went to discuss his portfolio. He never called again and had not been seen since. They lived together on and off. No children, no common property, no pictures of them together, no criminal record she knew of.

Gerald had his lawyer call Felicia to ask if it was true that Harry had died. She immediately hung up. On the second try, the lawyer told her that if Harry had promised to split the benefits with her if she filed a bogus claim, he might make it worth her while if she told him where Harry was. Felicia later went to see him. For the occasion, her hairdresser suggested middle-aged spikes around her head to convey a tired shocked look. Her lipstick was scarlet high gloss. Strangely, she thought white nurse's shoes would neatly match her outfit: a patterned sun dress. She received five thousand dollars for her trouble.

"When you see Harry, tell him the dirt on the streets of New York has more going for it than he does."

"Where is he," Gerald's lawyer asked.

"He's like the walking dead. He lies down occasionally to feed on the bottom. That's where you'll find him. Right at the bottom."

Normally, she was not a vindictive person. Felicia went out of her way to do something to Harry because that is what he would have done. Being paid for information was doubly sweet. All she had to do was talk and have smart people enjoy what she had to say. The money was a windfall and much needed. Her contribution gave medicinal value to a societal wound; and she could use her nurse's shoes for tennis, which she had yet to play.

At first Gerald did not know what to do with Harry's cell number. If Harry were dead, he could not be killed a second time. His original plan overcame his more unsavory instincts. Gerald prepared a file replete with pictures and biographical information of Harry, which he gave to the police. Harry was quickly found, arrested and charged with fraud. The arresting officers told him what he had done was worse than graveyard vandalism, a despicable display of greed. Harry was granted the right to post bail, claiming Felicia dreamt up the whole thing as an act of vengeance and a desperate attempt to discredit his good standing in the community.

Harry eventually worked out a plea bargain which reduced the charge to a misdemeanor. He paid a fine, no prison time. Gerald was at the court when the judge accepted the deal but told Harry he was a disgrace to the community.

"I have seen people do pretty low things because they had to survive, sir."

"Judge, that's me. I have to survive," Harry pleaded.

"I don't think that's your excuse. Why don't you just admit you prey on other people to satisfy your greed."

"I'm here without a lawyer. What if I admit that?"

"If you admit it, you're only doing it to manipulate me. You have a plea bargain. The prosecution thinks it's appropriate. I think it best to follow the prosecution. But in my eyes, there isn't a poop-scooper big enough for you."

A journalist dogged Harry outside along the sidewalk. Harry threw his half-filled coffee cup at him. The next day, the newspaper had a page 3 article on Harry, complete with his picture, home address, telephone numbers and license plate number.

Harry's story began to change once he saw the possibilities. He got the ear of a tabloid reporter to whom he related his adventure as one of the surviving roof surfers. Once he realized a plane had struck the floors below, he and several others had raced to the roof to await rescue. The stairwells were filled with panicked office workers, most of whom were racing in the opposite downward direction. Harry tried his best to direct the flow upward: he just could not be heard above the tremendous noise of human fear, cell phones, clacking shoes and thunder below. He was lucky, he said, not to have been knocked over by the vortex of people spiraling toward the lower floors. Sheer strength and a tight grip on the railing got him to the top landing, where he found the door open. After negotiating his way through the mechanical room full of ductwork and air control machinery, he saw someone overhead disappear into skylight. Harry figured it was the opening to the roof he had been seeking and managed his way finally to the outside.

As soon as he was on the roof, he spotted five, ten, twenty people who had made the journey, standing together at the base of one of the massive air conditioning ducts. As he made his way toward them, the structure shook so violently it knocked him over, causing him a head injury. TThe tower beam collapsed, leaving him flattened on his back, as if he were on the floor of a high-speed elevator, or better, a wide surf board taking a trough.

And that's how he survived: he surfed down a hundred plus floors, got up covered in dust, and picked his way out of the debris. His head wound had caused him such severe amnesia he only came to months later while everyone thought he was dead.

Chapter 13

Soldier Price

At age twenty-one, enraged, Price enlisted in the army. Gerald insisted he seek out the officer corps.

"All the planes I used to fly are in the museum. War is now a computer game. If that's the way you have to fight, doesn't matter as long as you fight. Seeing you in a uniform makes me feel like I'm fighting through you. Boy, I'm mad."

"I'll come back with a good story," Price said.

The skills Price emphasized were marksmanship and computers. The recruiter quickly streamed him into special unit training, especially given the quality of his English and his declared desire to fix the bad things in the world. He passed the colour test by consistently writing that blue was his favorite. The same with the animal test: lions, panthers and ibexes. He was solid in every way, deferential and clearly eager to give his devotion to the chain of command.

"If I told you to kill an enemy soldier, would you do it?"

"That's my job, sir," Price quickly replied.

"If he was a prisoner of war, would you kill him if ordered?"

"An order is an order, sir."

"You stopped to think, didn't you?" the recruiter said.

"I'm not in the situation, sir." Price answered.

"You will be. What are you going to do then?"

"I'm here to follow orders, nothing else." Price said.

Price excelled, even though some of his superiors were younger than he. He accepted orders with military enthusiasm. His marksmanship while a teenager with a .22 caliber rifle proved to be useless. He should have spent more time in a paintball maze, tripping, ducking and falling in active maneuvers. In fact, he realized his deficiencies lay in his knowledge of foreign languages, car mechanics and playing with knots. Within weeks, though, he was fixing bugs in intelligence computers. After a few months, he was sent for a half-year tour of duty to Afghanistan.

Gerald was more than proud of him. If he had ever felt guilty of thinking of him as a son, he saw there was no reason for it. For the occasion, he hosted a small party for Price. Gerald put on his old uniform; Price wore his; and the resulting pictures showed they both had the same smile.

"Price, you have never given me any advice. Maybe you thought it was not your place. I've learned so much from you, more than I could ever teach you."

"Well, now that you mention it, I do have a piece of advice for you. Keep being the best grandpa anyone ever had. You've protected me all my life. Now I'm going to the other end of the world to protect you."

Most of the action he saw was flushing out caves. With a small unit under him, he located target mountain ridges mainly east of Tora Bora, scouted out precipices closer to the Pakistani border, and thought up ways to determine if the enemy was hiding inside the mountain or in the huts of the local Pashtun. The topographical maps were excellent, showing the sweep of the solemn and deadly mountain ridges. Most of the more valuable information was gleaned on night patrol, watching against the full moon for smoke or movement, and lying in wait with infra-red night equipment and metal detectors.

Nothing in the landscape was trustworthy. The horizon was obscured by the peaks, meaning that the sun still lurked for hours before setting, even though it had disappeared from the visible sky. What seemed to be a human echo was the wind traveling over bushes and ledges, and bouncing off the faces of cliff-sides. Birds or bats would energetically strafe their helmets for no evident reason. Barrenness was easily confused with hostility. Price would not have been surprised if a live dinosaur strode through the unfamiliar vista trailed by a family brood.

The greatest peril next to mines was loose rock. His unit had trained in the North American deserts, and theoretically the terrain in parts was equivalent. Stones, pebbles, chips, silt giving way underfoot sent out a message to the enemy of danger and imminence. There was no way to avoid it. Even the mountain goats kicked out rock as they scrambled from ledge to thinner ledge.

"Don't think those goats are stupid," he told his unit. "They never slip off the cliff. Ever see a dead goat at the bottom of the canyon? They know where to find food. They know where to find water. And if I were a terrorist hiding in a cave, I'd like to be near one of these animals so I could learn from it and eat it."

Sometimes they planted a listening device delivered by high-powered cross-bow. It detected human or large mammal movement, and the depth of penetration. When suspicion warranted, one soldier sent in smoke bombs, or live grenades.

The problem was avoiding a landslide over the mouth of the cavern. Infrequently, the explosives found a cache of munitions, triggering a momentous belch of fire, smoke and debris. In some previously undetected fissures they found human remains, or water canteens and cans of food.

Price looked at the pocks in a ridge along the Spin Range. Some had been naturally carved by years of temperature change and water movement. Others had been carved by men, or enlarged and deepened by them recently or during other wars in past eras. If he had his choice, he would have sealed them all in order to restore the mountain face. It bothered him that things were borrowing into the mass of stone like worms in a book. Animate life did not belong inside the cliffs: it should have decorated the outside projections or curvatures, like the many bushes, nests and toupees of moss on sporadic terraces.

His unit managed to kill dozens found in two adjoining caves. Some died in the initial detonations, while others put up a fire-fight as they poured out of the holes, without a chance of surviving.

They rarely found a wounded man. Once they did, a fighter on the verge of death, stained in blood and dirt from his head to lower abdomen. His body was lying in an odd position, on its side, the head on rock, so if the man was casually reclining in a bed, about to turn over to see who had just come into his room. He was babbling between gasps, completely unintelligible. Price stood over him, thinking he was an intelligence asset if only he could be kept alive. He died moments later, in the same position, on a bed of rocks, a creature, a beast, a large piece of difficult vegetation.

The next night, they found another one of the enemy, barely breathing, who had the pulse of a leaf vein. He also died while Price looked down on him. The man was leaning against a bush in a bloodied crouched position, as if he were hiding behind it. Death came to him crouched, an unusual greeting, a strange departure, holding his knees and his pain together with the ligature of his arms. Grenades hung from his belt like ripe, dark avocados, the fruit he had packed for heaven.

Price double-checked the body count. Many of the dead had no recognizable faces, which led him to ask himself what he was counting. They were packages without address labels, or remaindered books without covers. They had lost their value because of their lack of identity. The dead were buried by the tribesmen who showed up after each battle to clean up the landscape. All the gravesites bore martyrs' flags. When the winds came, the flags made a clapping noise, a tireless applause across a still stage.

Price had little emotion to expend on the ones he had killed. Their death was a consequence of the role they chose to play. They filled in the Malthusian theorem, which did not consider it necessary to quantify revenge or hatred. That the evil died for their evil deeds was recorded as the need for the world population to regulate itself in the face of limited resources. For that reason, he expressly forbade any soldier from cutting off fingertips or ears of the dead as a trophy. The rules of war were even stricter that those of civil society. The idea of a souvenir was repugnant because recalling the stress of the situation at a later date would be so painful.

The army as an enterprise was no different than any commercial business. It had one advantage over a commercial structure: the ideology was not false or hypocritical. Price was angry, yet anger was not the army's ideology and he understood it. There was no question that the army had as its goal the protection of the society out of which it was recruited. The currency was the giving of orders and their execution.

No-one would ever say of any national army that it was hypocritical in aligning itself with national security, whatever it might be. No-one would accuse one nation's army of working in fact for an enemy country. Certainly there were corrupt army officials, insubordinate soldiers within the ranks, spies at various levels. But as a body, an army could seek to destroy its own nation, perhaps a governing regime, but never the nation itself. Machiavelli's aversion to permitting a foreign army to take up residence in a host state grew out of the experience that soldiers have no allegiance but to their motherland, and view other nations as places to conquer, occupy, neutralize or exploit. How good a soldier is depends on his training and commitment to his superiors. How solid his commitment is depends on his training. How solid his commitment to his own country is depends on his sensibility as a citizen. One soldier in his unit was a bed-wetter. Another continually cried during fire-fights. But those quirks did not stop or disqualify them from their duty.

Price suffered only one casualty. She was the only woman in the unit. Her wedding band and locket picture of her husband, a sergeant, were enough to keep most men from hitting on her. When that did not dissuade, as in the case of one soldier who stalked her, she removed her false front tooth. She also carried a small vial of animal excrement which she was ready to crack, but did not have to. Price valued her because of her acute sense of hearing and smell. She was able to tell whether the configuration of the landscape was regular, or whether rocks had been displaced or some recent human intervention had left an innocuous hint. One morning, she refused to get out of her sleeping bag even though the curl of her body looked as if she had been struggling for some minutes to get out of it. Her face was covered in dark dirt, as if she had just applied a mud pack for a beauty treatment. Her hair was flecked with bits of grass, miniature twigs and a slow beetle. Maybe it was due to the sexual assault days before; or her near death in planting a mine, or for that matter, the snap sandstorm. She was now useless to Price, and worse, a liability to herself and the rest of the soldiers. Once she was discharged, Price had no reason to follow-up on her well-being.

Unpacking a package of machine gun parts freshly removed from their crate, Price found a folded card, hole-punched and tied with a plastic thread to a clip. The card turned out to be the manufacturer's warranty. *'Satisfaction granted for the lifetime of this product'.* It warned him to fill out the return-mail card to record the user's name. One of the parts fit too loosely in the gun, and not because it was over-oiled. Price was afraid to have one of his men fire the weapon, so he rigged up the gun with a trigger string as it was wedged between a few stones. The recoil sent the loose part flying sideways which would have seriously maimed any soldier holding the weapon.

That night, Price took an hour out of his sleep to write a letter to the manufacturer detailing the incident, complaining about the immorality of shipping defective parts (*"Someone could have been killed"*) and asking how satisfaction could be guaranteed if the worker who tooled the part was either lazy or dishonest. Within a month, he received a reply from the office of the manufacturer's president regretting that he felt the way he did and that its responsibility was limited to replacement of the part.

When his tour of duty was up, he returned home and enlisted within a month for duty in Iraq.

Price was told in acclimatization sessions that his best friend was his gun. He had heard that before. He had not previously heard what one officer said:

"Imagine you're in Times Square on New Year's Eve. Everyone's laughing because something happy is about to take place. Shift to Times Square in Baghdad. Everyone around you is laughing because they're waiting to kill you or themselves or because nothing is going to happen until they decide. Happy New Year, soldier."

It was the same message Price had for Chazy. She never expressed doubt about his desire to serve his country. She did ask him for circumspection, for a commitment to come back alive; and if he could not give that commitment, to make a choice between her and his country. Price said the best he could do was to promise to love her more than before. Beyond that simple expression, he was powerless. The magnetic forces dragging events across the world stage also dragged him. They held his heart in a specially designed net and pulled the rest of him along.

The terrain had shifted to something less brutal, and although there were less competing tribes, the battles in Fallujah, sectors of Baghdad, and Mosul were more vicious than Price had experienced before. Roadside and car bombs were indiscriminate, as were dope-crazed suicide bombers in the middle of marketplace crowds. The colours of blood and sand mixed well. Blood on civilian clothing was so common to the soldier called to a scene that it looked as if sprayed by a designer. Murder any time any place rode up every defenceless street like a morning hawker of pita breads. Those who had reveled in the 9/11 attack and the bus bombings in Jerusalem found a larger constituency on which to practice in Iraqi hotels, road intersections, police stations and open-air markets.

Price hunted the enemy but did not know where to find him. In the Afghan mountains, he sensed where to go and merely had to wait out the enemy. Urban guerilla or terrorist warfare bore no analogy because of street corners. Turning a corner could be fatal, as was walking from day into night. Houses could not be trusted; fig vendors and those with inventories of souvenirs postcards were maliciously hostile behind those smiling corrupted teeth. There was no toe-hold, no absolutely safe wall against which to lean a soldier's back. Looters were always on call once someone was half or thoroughly dead after an explosion in broad daylight. At least hell had a hierarchy which everyone respected.

What disturbed Price most was the visit from politicians from home. Those who suddenly appeared in military fatigues for their half hour stay were excusable; those who showed up in suits without ties were not. A civilian in charge of defense or foreign affairs should have looked the part: impeccable double-breasted generous lapels bordering a golden or red-blue tie clasped around a very starched white collar. Removing the tie was not a sign of being casual: it was an insult. An official by definition is not casual. He is only credible when he looks official. This is the rule of clothing which Price promulgated when a small delegation of senators came to camp. When asked to speak freely by one delegate, he told him he must wear a tie around soldiers. The senator found the remark odd, if not hostile, and mentioned it to Price's superior and the other politicians. The head of the delegation approached him to ask if everything was all right. Price glared at his open shirt, which made him step back and move on to the next handshake.

Price sat at the back of the jeep next to the gunner. Everyone's boots were dusty from dirt and dust on the floor of the vehicle. The jeep had not been washed for weeks. Their route once a day took them through embassy row, consisting of ample streets lined with walled extravagant villas, cement blocks, curled razor-wire and occasional downed branches of palms.

The zone looked unkempt and lazily impressive. The size of the barricading installations in front of the buildings testified to the hint of magnificence of décor, wall hangings, even wood-work in the colonial-era buildings behind them. For the most part, junior staff occupied the compounds, many local strangers who felt comfortable enough not to be a target. Ambassadors were either back home in their countries of origin or with a growing contingent of colleagues in Jordan. Whatever traffic there was, crawled. Whoever was on the street felt the scrutiny of many eyes, the cross-hairs of several sights.

In one swing-through, a man in a white suit, tie-less, wide-brimmed hat, suspender-less, shouted out in slow-accented English, "Can I throw you a flower!"

The gunner swiveled toward him, and Price raised his gun, as the pedestrian gently swung his arm back and let fly a short-stemmed rose. The soldiers were braced for the worse until they saw the trajectory of the object. They released their tense fingers as the rose dropped into Price's lap. The jeep stopped, permitting Price to jump out and run toward the man. He was standing half in the sun and half in the shade caused by the interference of the corner of a roof with the direct line of the sunlight.

"Are you crazy? We could have shot you!"

"Then you would have shot me over a flower," the man said. The brim of his hat covered most of his eyes.

"You do not throw things at soldiers, sir!" Price shouted again. He could not understand his calmness. "Identification papers, sir."

"Take them out of my jacket pocket, soldier. I am passport attaché at the embassy."

Price quickly verified his statement from his diplomatic documents. The driver in the jeep called to Price to wrap things up.

"Do not do that again, sir. And you should not be on the open street."

"You can call me Frederik, soldier."

The next day, they drove by the same spot. The man was there, in no hurry to do his business. The line between sunlight and shade was so well defined it was sharp; so sharp that toes on one side and heel on the other felt different heat. He stood on it, as if it were carved in the concrete, capable of being filled in with sand, or paved over to obliterate the distinction. Nothing else on the street or in the air was so definitive.

"Hey soldiers, can I throw you a feather?" he shouted.

Again they tensed up as he threw a seagull's feather in the air in their direction.

Price rushed him, pushing him against the sandstone villa wall behind him.

"What is it with you, Frederik? Do you have a death wish?"

"Then I have a death wish, my own but not yours," the official said.

"Do not talk to us. Do not throw things at us. We kill people for making a wrong move. You've been lucky so far."

"Soldier, I have been in worse places. I have been in the Congo. I have been in Bosnia, in Tiananmen Square..."

Price released him, startled, staring at him in silence.

"There is no sense to how the world works, you know. The rule of law is just tension. Conflict is natural. Peace is wind and war is wind."

"I disagree Frederik. Watch yourself."

"Price could not see his eyes because of Frederik's hat. He quickly bent down slightly; Frederik tilted his hat downward. Price was tempted to knock his hat off.

Over the next few days, the official was on their route, calling to them and lobbing a flower or showering them with confetti. The gunner told Price he didn't trust him, that the next thing he would throw is a grenade. He thought if the official was suicidal, he might take them with him.

On their last day of patrol in that area, Price got out of the jeep before it went down the street and snuck up behind Frederik. Price saw the gray hair at his neck was trimmed.

"What's in your hand, sir?" Price asked placing the end of his gun at Frederik's back.

"Nothing. I have no flowers today. I have no feathers. This morning I went to the barber's shop for my usual shave. The shop was no longer there. Blown up. No hot towels for my face. No lime after-shave. Not even a chair. Not even my barber. Today, I was just going to wave."

"Good idea."

Frederik looked at him with something less than desolation, more than resignation.

"You are not the complaint department, are you soldier?"

"No sir. There are official channels for complaints."

"And if I went through official channels, I suppose you could help me with my problem in a few months or years."

"The only problem I see here is you're causing delay to this patrol, sir. You should stay inside where you belong."

"My problem is I don't trust anyone or anything. Can you fix that?"

"Official channels, sir."

"I am leaving. This place is not a country, only a history. I am being transferred to the United Nations. The heart of hypocrisy. Maybe I will see you on the streets of New York City. I am going from the capital of hell to the capital of diplomatic heaven."

Price ran to his jeep as it came up. Around the next block, a parked car exploded, killing the driver who triggered the explosion and four pedestrians. When Price's jeep got there, the ghosts of the dead were rising from the disassembled bodies, knowing a second explosion would imminently kill those who came running to the rescue. They did not know the directions to Frederik's hell or heaven and assumed that by hovering on the spot, someone, anyone, would be kind enough to greet them.

It was those ghosts Price spoke to as he tried to sleep at night in the barracks. His position was clear: chaos and randomness exist as a temporary phenomenon like the clutter of building materials at a construction site. They soon become immured as the structure is built. All of the reasons physics gives for violent dissociation of incompatible elements conspire to create order, stability and a foundation of predictability. The ghosts claimed that their host bodies had been terminated by that chaos. Chaos, for them, was permanent. The only possible argument against the permanence of randomness was that death created stability and ended suffering. Price disagreed, saying that sometimes perspective magnified what was a grain of sand into a mountain range.

Beyond that, what else could be said? The war was a job carried out with hatred of person, but not with hatred of person. While most jobs added value to a social endeavour, being a soldier in a conflict zone directly added that value. Killing the enemy ended the enemy's tyranny. Finding the enemy helped kill him. Correcting the world had little to do with an inspired word or an impeccable study on a focus group. Poets were not the unsung legislator any more than the scientist was a visionary. What was out of place in the world had to be put back in place. Movement required energy. Energy was the sister of force.

Chapter 14

Price In Public

Once Price left the army, he resumed his career in software investment. He committed himself intensely as if it were a calling, as his destined contribution to the evolution of the human spirit. He was refreshed in the same way a cleaner is refreshed after mopping to a shine the concourse at a train station. He had mopped up evil people, manned roadblocks to catch toxic infiltrators and laid the foundations for the next cycle of guardians of the peace. Fulfillment had replaced anger. Chazy was as welcoming and supportive as ever, and urged her not to let him take her for granted.

For weeks after his return, he felt naked without a weapon. His baseball cap seemed too flimsy a replacement for his helmet. He could not wade into a crowded mall or hotel lobby without spotting, scanning and scouting. Price refused to go into a movie theatre with Chazy.

"Aside from you, who is really sitting near me in the dark?"

His caution, which she called his understandable paranoia, extended to skipping a few turns on escalators and looking behind him on the stairs. He would take the next elevator and the next taxi in line. Cell phone use became questionable.

Strangers had secrets either in their minds or somewhere within their clothing. It disoriented him not to be able to stop and search a messenger service van moving at walking speed as he made his way along the sidewalk. The policemen on their beat leaning against their parked car looked so unconcerned about their surroundings, they would easily have been targets for snipers. Price felt the air was crisp, while no one else felt it to be anything other than warm and very ordinary air. Nothing was about to happen even though Price felt a click, a crash, an explosion might befall the unguarded at any time.

Chazy submitted his name as a panelist at the World Trade Conference. He was readily accepted and was even asked to lead the discussion on hi-tech entrepreneurship. Chazy arranged for the preparation of a power-point presentation instead of a formal speech. The organizers were very interested in having a business, not an academic voice, leading the panel. Although he had never before spoken publicly on his views, they assumed he would take a conservative stance in view of his entrepreneurial background. Price was surprised she had made the submission without his knowledge.

"Recently, you've been like a side of beef that needs moving around."

"How do you know I'm not busy on that day?"

"I have your empty agenda, and besides, you're speaking in Switzerland."

The day the organizing committee sent out its publicity, Price spotted an e-mail in his screen with an attachment he sensed was a virus. The message, though, mentioned his name.

"Price DeMann, think you're going to globalize? See you in the streets."

The sender was Trix, of course no-one he knew. He deleted the e-mail.

Two more came that week from the same sender, each inviting him to reply and explain dogmatically why local economies and cultures were being destroyed because money-men wanted to homogenize world markets. All signed Trix. Price forwarded the last e-mail to one of his little-used computers and opened the attachment. It contained a fuzzy picture of Trix, which could have been a portrait of a mottled tennis ball. Several press clippings and links indicated he was a one-course student in New York, and a "left-wing protest organizer with a long list of arrests".

Price replied: "Imagine my joy when I received your delightful messages. What will you be wearing for the occasion, designer or off-the-rack?"

The response was swift: "Chartreuse, you f... "

The e-mail discussion continued every few days for weeks. Both toned down their edge, especially after Trix apologized for not writing the day before.

"Both my grandmothers died yesterday. Same old age, different old age homes. Like they got together to say *"How come Trix hasn't visited for five years?"* It threw me. You can't throw me, though."

Price did not know what to make of the non-doctrinaire confession.

"Sorry for your loss. Can't argue with death."

Trix rebounded days later. His e-mail contained a mixture of fonts, starting with Arial, progressively with each paragraph moving through fonts with more tails and swirls. There was no purpose to it except to provide a sub-script or a subtle edge to a simple response. Trix, for all his cynicism, was committed to depth and to showing it off. Like every organizer or point man, he had his sycophants who loved the action with all their thin being. He would have preferred not to have a retinue, yet one man alone could not make a phalanx, or a parade. He had enough sense of mission to fill several bodies. Trix was said to be all over the place. Nothing, though, could replace a loyal army.

"I went from one funeral in Brooklyn to another in New Jersey. You know what. Same chain of funeral homes. Same service and casket prices. You can't argue with death if there's only one franchise."

In reply to Price's question about "what's eating you?", Trix wrote: "Agro-business is eating me. The North American way of life is eating up the rest of the world, me included."

"What's really eating you?" Price replied.

"Same old thing." Trix responded immediately. "My right foot is one size bigger than the other. I'm a size 10 and 11. When I was a kid, my mother had to buy two pair of shoes just so I could wear one. My parents didn't have money to burn like some people I know. I would stuff a rag into my left shoe to fit me into the bigger size. I felt like a left-footed clown. No sympathy from the shoe stores, the big chain stores who could afford to break sizes for me. No two-for-one sales for my family either. Good thing my hands are the same size. Otherwise, I would hate the mitten guys."

The last of his twenty e-mails soured. It contained three happy-face icons.

"Hope I wasted a lot of time you could have been spending exploiting and pillaging. Get ready to sic your dogs on me." The rest of his message was typed in capital letters.

"By the way, I personally know a Marine who was shot in the leg and now is limping for life. You know what he does? He sells furniture. He has to limp back and forth from the customer to the manager to make the sale, and he gets minimum wage and a bloody commission. They didn't want him for an army desk job because they thought it would take him too long to limp from his chair to the office cooler. You know what he did? He changed his name to Elvis."

Price wrote back in a six-point font: "Maybe your Marine shot himself."

Trix was not only busy organizing and fuming. At night he worked without fanfare as a part-time paleontologist analyzing dinosaur stools for a private consulting group on contract with the museum. He wrote articles in the professional journals detailing his findings and the theories he constructed on the rise and disappearance of the creatures based on the remnants of their diet. He traveled extensively in the Midwest picking up samples at county fairs and souvenir shops along the road. Several of the so-called dinosaur poop patties sold were really baked mud cakes confected by unscrupulous sellers. Most people did not know the true scientific value of the remnants, which were sometimes more telling than the popular skeletal remains.

If he were pressed, he would have to admit that his concept of law stemmed from the awe he had for the massive creatures he studied. This was not a Hegelian approach at all. They had defined their own law based on need, breed and instinct. Law was an emanation of the ruling class, and had no other function than to detail the desire of the ruler to continue ruling. It was static, and tolerated no dissent which threatened the status quo. The cakes of reptilian manure he analyzed were a codification of dinosaur law in that what it ate described its maker's entitlement and everything else's disentitlement. Unlike many children, Trix had no desire to be a dinosaur or to meet one. He assumed it had no personality except for its weight, size and eating habits. If it was socially committed, its loyalty was limited to its family, which did not interest him.

Price was annoyed with himself for having wasted time on Trix's e-mails. After reading the last one, he got into his car and drove on the highway for an hour with the window open in order to have the wind slap his face. As he returned, he saw a Labrador retriever running slowly on the shoulder of the highway, trailing a leash. The dog kept glancing behind as if waiting for its master to stop and scoop it up. It was obvious to Price the dog would soon be run over. He came to a stop on the shoulder ahead of the dog, opened the passenger door and waited for the animal to jump in. It did just that.

Price rolled the passenger window down to permit occupants of passing vehicles to see the dog and claim it. He drove as slowly as was safe, but without success.

Once he returned to the city, he drove to the animal shelter and deposited the dog. Price had saved its life on the highway only to deliver it to a home where it would probably be put down within days. His adventure had been a definite benefit for the flow of traffic. It has otherwise been a waste of time for the dog.

Chazy was telling Price she was expecting when Napanee and Cheryl walked into his office. He was as ecstatic as she had hoped him to be when he heard.

"What a charming couple! Cheryl, notice how Chazy is always so well coordinated. Do you have two pleats in your skirt? Price, I have to talk to you about my deal. I have matching funding. Everything has come together. I want you on my side."

Price looked at his wife, who took the cue.

"We have an announcement... I'm pregnant," she said, measuring her words.

Napanee said she hoped it went well and immediately asked Price to make a decision.

Price again looked at Chazy, whose face said she had not expected more from his mother.

"Yes. I've come to a decision. The first pre-condition to letting you know what it is, is that you give Chazy a big hug."

Napanee thought he was joking. She had never said much to Chazy before or since the marriage. Her father made sure to take care of her. Mother and daughter-in-law rivalry did not exist, since their contact had not solidified into a relationship. For that matter, her relationship with Price over the years had not grown or matured because she had put no effort into it. Asking her to hug Chazy, though, struck her as a command to swear subservience. Maybe it was the intonation, or the fact that Cheryl was in the room. It was a declaration of disrespect, like ordering her to serve a dog as a sacrifice to a false god.

"I'm not hugging anyone until you tell me what you want me to do with this."

Napanee withdrew from her purse a colorized picture of Price as a one-year old standing inside a carpeted bathtub, his arms hanging over the rim, his fingers almost touching the top of a pile of books next to it. He had not seen the picture before.

"What do you want to do with it?" he asked.

"Give it to a collector for a million bucks."

Napanee had not noticed, and now that she did, was relieved. Cheryl was gently swiveling in one of the chairs, idly looking through her credit cards.

"I've been saving that bathtub in mini-storage for years. What for? I always asked myself. If my own son, who should hold a childhood legacy so dearly, doesn't want it, why am I paying warehousing fees?"

"How much do you really want for it?"

"If you don't want to invest with your mother, I can understand. Just tell me. I'll make other arrangements. I'm not insulted, am I, Cheryl?"

Chazy mourned briefly. The opportunity to bring Napanee into her family came and went like an un-hailed taxi. She had never met a person like her mother-in-law, whom she would have wanted to describe as cold. She was not cold: simply disconnected.

Shortly after the birth of Chazy's son, Cheryl saw that Napanee could not figure out how to connect, so she sent Chazy a gift. She bought two baby knit outfits, pink and blue, and shipped them to her with a card that read:

"You choose and send me back the one you want."

The next day, Chazy received a call from Cheryl who asked where she could deliver her fruit basket.

"Who's the fruit for?"

"For you, Chazy. It's got good stuff for the baby, like passion fruit and dried mango. And not a lot of cellophane."

Whatever the impact of the news of pregnancy, it did not show in Napanee's face nor her language, except that she asked Cheryl to deal with it. After the perfunctory exchange with Chazy, Cheryl thought she had done what she had to. What remained in her mind was the extra gravity of nascent motherhood she caught in Chazy's voice, like picking up a hidden accent. She did not know what to do with that accent, surprised that she even caught it. Cheryl imagined it came from a tiny voice within, the same voice she had experienced when she was pregnant. For days it bothered her until she developed a sympathetic swelling in her own belly. The distension must have been caused by a bad bean salad or strong cheese she bought at a farmer's market.

Cheryl noticed through Chazy that time had passed. Her belly was now reacting in dismay to that passage. She became so frustrated by the end of the week that she told her husband, with whom she had not been intimate for years, "Do not touch me. You dare touch me, you're out of the house," she said as she hovered behind him.

He was reading the newspaper spread out on the kitchen table and had just handed her a carton of milk.

"What's the problem, dear?" he asked, looking up from the obituary page.

"You know why I got pregnant, don't you?"

"You mean why, or clinically?"

"I was stupid. I let you invade me. I had no self-respect. And you always wore your undershirt."

"How else do you make kids, dear? Aren't you happy with our kids? What's the problem this morning?" he answered.

"I don't want to be pregnant again. Do you understand me?"

"Little chance of that. Unless you're fooling around with the milkman."

"Don't be funny. We're having a serious conversation."

Cheryl pulled the newspaper away from him. She asked if he was fooling around.

"I turned off when you turned off."

"I don't believe you. Men don't work that way."

"Divorce. Are you talking divorce?"

"I want to know. Look at me. I want to know if you have been taking advantage of me while I was sleeping."

"Are you all right, Cheryl?"

"If I'm pregnant…"

"If you're pregnant, you can get out of the house."

"Are you dense? If I'm not, then nothing's been happening. Nothing at all."

"And nothing will until we each die in our separate beds."

"That's a terrible thing to say."

"And if you die first, I wouldn't really know it because you told me not to touch you, and I couldn't shake your body to see if you were alive."

Cheryl pushed the newspaper back in front of him. She sat down, opened the clasp of her turtle-necked collar, whispered to him.

"Are you sure? While I was sleeping, the blanket falls off. You come over in the dark."

"And what? Jump on you? The house alarm would have gone off."

"I wouldn't trust you for a minute."

Napanee had other ideas. The growth inside Chazy was a predicament, like the formation of a disease. She felt uncomfortable around sick people, unsure whether to mention the sickness, or even simple regrets. How could she say anything meaningful to Chazy that could express her sympathy. All pregnancies were unwanted. There was no point to them except discomfort and there were already enough people in the world competing for bargains.

Chazy made a further effort. She sent Napanee a thank-you note for the fruit, and a small album of baby pictures. In a separate box delivered a week later, she enclosed a small envelope with a lock of the baby's hair attached to his birth photo. A little while later, Chazy shipped Napanee an envelope containing a copy of the baby's birth certificate and blue booties to give some life to the certificate.

"Why are you sending me all this stuff?" Napanee asked her over the telephone.

"To keep you current. You haven't seen him yet," Chazy said.

"What am I going to do with it," Napanee complained.

As was the case with previous economic summits, police expected and got anarchy in the streets of Geneva and confrontation with security forces. Price was scheduled to address an audience of young hi-tech businessmen and politicians at the same conference center where government leaders were meeting.

The demonstrations were organized in part by Trix, who invited him to a public debate in the square about a mile from the conference center.

That day, grandmothers linked arms, marched with European medical interns in operating gowns, sweat-banded nihilist students, old Maoists, civil liberty lawyers, Arctic-warming prophets, radical chefs and soccer-rowdies. None of them were Swiss; most had entered the country through Zurich as tourists interested in buying chocolates and doing some skiing. Several demonstrators and policemen had been injured in street fights. A guard horse had been stabbed with a picket sign. It was difficult to tell the journalists from the police. Most of the roofs were either populated by snipers or long-range cameramen.

Price was familiar with Geneva. Most modern political movements traced some seminal historical event to the city, the place where rifts were healed or confirmed over cocktails at a neutral site.

Those who came purely to do private business or banking did not want to be seen. Those who came to buy chocolates, ski or make the American news wanted to be seen. It was a false impression that the local population was unfriendly. Price described them as curt, impatient and unhelpful, based on his contact with shopkeepers, hoteliers and cab drivers. That did not immediately suit him because he considered the primary approach of strangers was to be welcoming. He encountered the same problem in Zurich, except for a street musician, not a Swiss citizen, who gave him directions.

Trix had written him the debate would last half an hour and focus on the issue of the Global Economy. "Bring your own security". The press releases being circulated by his ad hoc organization listed the debate as an "event".

Carrying a bull-horn, Price showed up at the soap-box stand in the square. A thousand demonstrators were milling around waiting for something to happen. Trix bounced up to the makeshift podium, nodded to Price, shouting: "Are you a capitalist?" Trix was clipped with a wireless microphone which was channeled to the monster speakers in the square. He introduced himself and introduced Price as the vanguard of the Young Conservative movement. As he spoke, his aides handed out press kits to the journalists hovering around the speakers. The crowd blew plastic trumpets, hissed and applauded as Trix's speech referred to what he called the bad people, the really bad people and the innocent minds people like Price wanted to corrupt.

After fifteen minutes, Price knew he was not going to have the opportunity to speak. He was there as a foil for Trix's invective. Price straightened his tie, walked in front of Trix. For the first time, he noticed his longish sideburns, one of them imitating an exclamation mark because of a round dark birth mark immediately below it. He stared as long as he could. Trix had mugged him and inadvertently saved his life on Wall Street. Trix must have been on drugs that day and could not now recognize him. Making a crucial decision that Trix was a negative, not positive force, Price hit him hard enough to knock him down. Priced pulled the microphone from Trix's shirt and stomped on it, causing the speakers to piercingly whistle. The intolerable shrillness was enough to force the evacuation of the square and permit Price to walk away hiding his bloodied fist in his pocket.

His walk turned to a run when he heard a small group chasing him, swearing. Although he was not out of the square, a blur of sweatshirts was still after him. Price ran in the street, next to moving traffic. One car seemed to be pacing him, a limousine driven by a formally dressed chauffeur, carrying one passenger. The window was rolled down, permitting the passenger wearing a white wide-brimmed hat to shout: "Want a ride?"

The chauffeur stopped the vehicle long enough for Price to open the door and jump in next to the driver's seat.

"Hooligans after you, young man?" the passenger asked.

"The freedom of speech is after me. Thank you for the ride."

"Did you just start a riot in the park? Your shirt and tie are enough to get them angry. Where shall we take you?"

"The Conference Center. I am on a panel of speakers this afternoon."

Price could not see the passenger because the seat was constraining. His voice, though, was accented, distinctive. He closed his eyes.

"Only diplomats and lobbyists do that."

"You are one hundred per cent correct."

Price moved forward toward the dashboard. Squirming around and with his knees now on the seat, he faced the passenger.

"You wouldn't know a consul named Frederik, would you?"

The passenger stared back from under his wide brim.

"You wouldn't know a soldier who would shoot people for throwing flowers?"

"I didn't, did I!"

"I was meaning to tell you something. Take offence if you like. There is no order in the world. I came across you not because it was destined. You escaped with your life just before because of the randomness of the chaos. The rule of law is the rule of coincidence. No one is reliable, and those who are, are for personal reasons."

"I've heard the same thing from people in despair."

"I'm not desperate. I like to think I'm experienced. This is your stop. Please be careful of lightning."

Chapter 15

Tolstoy and Gerald

When Tolstoy grew very old, his mind sought another reality. He took up shoe cobbling. Sitting on a box in front of a metal mould with scraps of leather, boot black, hammer and nails for heels, he insisted on repairing the boots of visitors.

Gerald's mind drove him to collect gloves: winter, gardening, mechanics, cleaning. He cut off the gloves' fingertips, which he then placed on his fingers. His hands looked as though they had been partially dipped in paint or excrement. Each fingertip had its own personality, the index being the most vivacious.

At first it seemed harmless. A business partner with whom he owned a small office building noticed Gerald's hands on the desk when it came time to sign a loan extension. He thought Gerald had done something to his fingers that required multiple bandages. The thimble-like coverings were different in colour and texture: they turned his digits into claws or hi-tech mini-missiles.

It became more serious when visitors found their gloves had been mutilated. During a lull in the conversation, he would go to the closet, pull a box cutter out of his trousers and operate on whatever he found in the coast pockets, even on mittens. Gerald was wearing their leather appendages on his fingers. He was otherwise normal, normal enough to resist Napanee's hints that they begin talking about his money.

"What I have is none of your business."

She knew enough to withdraw.

"Maybe one day it will be your business. Not as long as I can bend over and put my own shoes on."

"At least tell Price I need eighteen million dollars. You're the one blocking it, I know. You and he are ganging up on me. It's an investment. Price has lots more. Is this the way to treat a mother."

"You're making me tired, Napanee."

Maybe it was fatigue. Gerald found it increasingly difficult to bend, to pick up flat objects from the floor. Changing a tire in twenty minutes was no longer an option, or a remote possibility. He could not thread a needle: the hole was invisible, the thread's end too ragged and quivering. He forgot phone numbers and where he put the cell phone. Gerald called Napanee his mother in a moment of distraction, although the distraction worsened. Evening, for him, came at seventeen o'clock.

It only took months. Gerald was not dying. He was sloughing off his life through heavy breaths, shiverings and irregular eye movements. His soul was using those things to form a floating mattress inches from his body, where it could take up position and watch over its former encasement. When propped up, he could speak, although speaking contributed a lot of good material for the mattress.

"Where did you put the medals?" he asked.

"Where did you leave them?" Napanee asked.

"It's the same thing. Where are they?" he agitated.

"Why do you need them?"

"I have to die with them on. That's why I got them. They're of no use to anyone but me."

Gerald was bloated, as if he had been found in a river by a couple of fishermen casting their lines off a small rural bridge. His face was no longer narrow: his cheeks had ballooned to bursting. That alone made it difficult to understand whatever he was saying.

Price stayed with him at his bedside for days. Chazy could not get him to eat more than a few spoonfuls of mash. When Gerald was finally lifeless, Price kissed his hand, said goodbye, and returned home to write a eulogy.

Price mourned a father. There was no other father to mourn, no one who committed his vitality to him on a natural and consistent basis. He tried centering the eulogy on the deceased, not on himself. The speech sounded too personal, meaning childish in its uncluttered emotion. Price cried within himself until Chazy told him she wished he could cry more deeply.

The last thing Gerald said was a word, incoherent to Price, yet apparently satisfying to Gerald. It had two syllables, could have been the name of a person, or of a place or of a fruit. Napanee thought he was complaining about too much yogurt in his oatmeal. She had bought too much and wanted to use up as much as she could before the expiry date. On top of that, she thought she had bought sweetened vanilla: it turned out to be plain and sour. Maybe he was telling her to return it and get her money back, because he wasn't going to do it. Give back the yogurt, he said with his last concerned breath. That made no sense to Price, except that he knew when people are just about to die, they tend to worry about their appearance or the fact they forgot to turn off the light in the basement closet.

No, his grandfather must have been trying to reduce a lifetime message to two syllables, like Be Good or Be True or Be Wise. He was thinking ahead while keeping death waiting.

At the very moment of his death, he was unattended. Whoever had been with him had either left momentarily or had already ended his visit. There was no company to see him off, although he had a problem with company. People were there to witness, not assist. Gerald had been floating for days. Room in his state of mind and comfort were at a premium. Witnesses were a distraction. Hovering and hand-holding were off the topic.

"Can you imagine, Cheryl," Napanee recounted, "it was the first time I was in a room with a dead person. And he lays a curse on me. I'm going to turn into a container of expired yogurt unless I give it back to the store."

After the reading of the will in which Gerald left her his estate, Napanee returned the yogurt to the supermarket and got her money back after an ugly fight with the assistant manager. It was eaten, he said. It was spoiled, she said.

That night, the words of the argument floated upward into the stars, totally unobscured by clouds or city lights. The words formed a white ball the size of a giant marshmallow, and then compressed themselves into a pinpoint of sparkle joining the other stars. Gerald had never made a fuss about the Big Dipper, and had never told Napanee about it. On his last few days, he thought about the four elements and naturally brought his mind around to the forgotten stars. Bloated as he was, he could not make anyone understand he was beginning to see the navel of galaxies with his naked eye. So clear was his vision that the bequest to Napanee was conditional: she could not spend more than two hundred thousand dollars each year without Price's approval. His gaze broke through local stars, reaching right to the wall where the universe ends.

Harry never questioned his own mortality even though Gerald was now gone. After all, he had outlived him. The age difference was not an issue. Gerald was a force, ageless, on Harry's back. Now he stopped being there. On, off, that was Gerald's business, not his own. His own business was that he felt sluggish, declining from market participant to consumer, and below that inert level, to observer. Observer status meant he always had an appetite which he fed with sugar, and an attention span which was too ephemeral to measure.

Writing on the back of a restaurant flyer which he never sent to Gerald, Harry confided:

"You think I did something wrong. Well I didn't. You also think I can never fix it. Well I can and I don't want to. Why should I give you the satisfaction. You're not my father."

Harry always thought that restaurant flyer captured the essence of their relationship. With Gerald's death, Harry set out to look for the manifesto, hoping he had not thrown it out with the trash years ago.

Diagnosing Harry as having attention deficit disorder was like saying a squirrel, or humming bird or chicken had ADD because of its rapid movements. At heart, he was as nervous as a looter during a riot: there was so much to take, so little time, so much competition, so few to trust. His true desire was to be locked into a bank vault long enough to neatly place bills in a suitcase with wheels, and then leave through two feet of steel and concrete into a waiting taxi. He was not an approval-seeker unless he had to be to take what he needed.

Looking back, Harry thought Gerald was insane, fixated on causing him as much unmerited misery as he could. Not that he wanted to dwell too long on Gerald's maniacal pursuit of the good life for Napanee. What could Gerald really have hoped to get out of him? He knew how to find Harry one way or another. He recognized his patterns of behaviour, his idiosyncrasies, his voice over a bad phone connection. It was unbearable, like a mosquito sensing it was about to be swatted. Harry could not stand up to him because he had great means, was an old man and was so driven he could not be reasoned with. Besides, maybe Gerald was going to leave him a special, quirky bequest in his will to show Harry there were no hard feelings.

What did hold his attention was a German Shepherd with well-groomed fur sitting on the side of a skateboard ramp in the park watching teen-agers zip by. As they did, the dog would distinctly cough, "drag" or "speed up" or "get off". Harry listened as it dispensed its wisdom. When the dog noticed Harry to the side tuning in, it started heavily panting, and between breaths, told him, "Sue someone you love". This was startling advice from a German Shepherd. Harry asked, "Who?" The dog's nose twitched, shutting off the conversation.

A lawsuit was not an easy burden to carry. The articulation process, finding the right lawsuit, the investment of time in the whole package had to be pre-arranged and accepted. Just because a German Shepherd recommended it did not mean Harry had to listen to it.

"Free advice is worth what you pay for it." Harry intoned, making sure to repeat it the next time he came across the dog.

As soon as Harry collected the odd ends of his thoughts, he had his attorney send a letter to Price demanding three hundred million dollars. He claimed he was near bankruptcy while his son was worth millions. His lawsuit portrayed a lamentable, chronic indigence on his part, an unfeeling and distant son he had tried to raise but could not because of interference by

Price's mother and grandfather, and a debt his son owed him for having introduced him to the profitable world of computers. It chronicled Harry's devastating fall from good fortune through bad investments and the moral hurt he suffered daily in being deprived a visit to his own grandson whom he had yet to see. All he wanted was reconciliation and the ability to meet his personal budget in dignity.

When that amount did not arrive one month later, he wrote to Price to advise him he would take ten million: he needed the money right away. When no response came after two weeks, Harry fired his lawyer without paying him and wrote again to Price, conceding he was a hard bargainer. As a man with many debts and approaching old age, Harry could not settle for less than one hundred million. Harry was not a fool. The letter was hand-written on cheap photocopy paper with a ball-point pen. The stamp on the envelope was licked and placed misaligned with the edges. Occasionally, the script in the letter was shaky, although generally confident. If the letters c and n were malformed out of haste, he wrote over them to make them more legible. These stood out when one first glanced at the paper, looking like sporadic ball-point blueberries embedded in every third or fourth sentence. These too conveyed the message he wanted to express.

Harry finally did get an answer from Price's lawyer, who had been Gerald's family attorney for years and who had grown in his legal practice with the stories of sporadic sightings and intrigues involving Harry. They had a meeting at the office after Harry signed a document attesting he was acting on his own behalf and had no desire to be assisted by counsel.

"Don't you serve coffee here? I need a tumbler-size coffee with sugar and froth. Can your secretary get me one?"

The lawyer said there was no time for coffee.

"There's always time to pause and put your face into a cup of steaming coffee. How about it?"

"How about you get one after you leave the office?"

The lawyer's pot-like head looked especially metallic in the bolts of sun coming through the windows and bouncing up from the glass surface of his desk. Harry tried not to look at his face: his robotic features betrayed no vestige of living skin. His hands were large spatulas, fingers stiff, as if they used to be in tight kitchen mittens. As he concentrated on his fingers, his host stared gravely through him.

"Mr. Souply, we are here to discuss what the future holds for you."

Harry was surprised.

"No we're not. We're here to see how much money my son should be paying me, seeing that I'm destitute."

The lawyer continued at the same grave rhythm.

"Mr. Souply, there is no proof you are the father of Price DeMann. There is no proof you are destitute. There is no law in the circumstances that permits you to ask for alimony from him."

"Wait a minute. There's no way you're telling me he's not my son. He has my face, my nose and eyes. What are you saying?"

"He does not look anything like you, Mr. Souply. He looks entirely like his mother and his grandfather and everyone else on that side of the family. Actually, he looks more like me and all my relatives than he does you."

Neither one shifted in their seats. To do so would have been an admission of lack of confidence. Some might have interpreted it as a signal that the shifter had better things to do. Harry wanted to get out of his seat and tear the diplomas off the wall. Maybe he would do that later.

"Why did you tell me to come here?"

"If you are prepared to be reasonable, we might be able to work things out."

Harry lifted himself slightly above his seat in a show of his ability to be attentive.

"What do you have in mind?"

"If you give me a complete list of your assets, income and debts on a running basis going back five years, an audited list, and if you undertake to update that list every quarter going forward, we are prepared to give you an allowance in partial payment of your rent and food."

"Rent and food?"

"One thousand dollars per month, subject to review."

"On thousand?... Are you kidding?... The kid is rich! Rich! What's a thousand bucks?"

The lawyer looked even more gravely at him: "Five minutes to accept the offer," he said.

"I don't need five minutes. I need five million dollars. Like right now."

"I assume that is a 'no'. Your way out is the same way you came in."

Harry stood up so that he was in a better position to shout a profanity. On his route to the door, he solidly kicked the hat stand which had no hats on it. It had had none hanging on its arms for at least fifteen years. Before that, people used to hang baseball caps and birthday hats on it, when it lived in a residential garage.

This is not what Harry had expected. Ten million in one shot was perhaps unreasonable and needed some imagination. A million down, and a half a million every year until he was curled up and diapered in a terminal hospital bed were what he should have received. The implication that he was not Price's father trickled down the spongy matter of his stomach. That was as devastating as telling him he was really left-handed, or that he had a twin brother and that both he and his twin had been adopted.

He could always deal with the increasingly tangible approach of death by seriously looking for a rich woman to marry. Harry would bring world-class experience and wisdom, while she would bring a portfolio to the marriage. The problem with rich women was that they were demanding; and at this stage of life, he had no patience to be answerable.

The issues were beyond resolution. Harry was bursting yet did not want to burst. Although his car only had half a tank of gas, he drove out of the city to cool off to no particular destination, looking at signs as they passed as a novelty. After a two hour drive, he found himself on the shores of a large lake. The country houses looked abandoned for the season and he had no trouble pulling a rowboat into the water. He rowed until he reached the opposite shore, where, to be constructive, he picked up rocks of various sizes and sparkles and placed them in the boat. On his way back, he felt intense pain in his shoulders as he rowed. Once on home shore, he saw the same rocks half in and half out of the water. Gerald shouted from the cedar deck of the house: "Who told you to put rocks on the bottom of my boat?"

"You're dead, what do you care?" Harry answered smartly.

"Rocks are now my friends. They don't belong in the boat."

"How do you know that?"

"The rocks told me. The boat told me. Get the hell out of there before I get them after you."

Chapter 16

Mayor Price

Since Price's purchase of the forested hill, the town at its foot-hill had expanded to meet the needs of the weekend skiing crowd. A one-acre lodge went up, followed by a number of A-frame cottages and two woodsy motels. A secondary road passing by his property was upgraded, a portion of the cost later appearing on his tax bill. There could not have been more than three thousand permanent residents in and around the town, although on the weekends and during the summer months, the transient tourist population swelled that number.

Price and Chazy had picked out a western-facing prom-ontory at the edge of their land to build a house. According to the plans, most of the façade was to be glassed, highlighted by a low-rise of grey field stones and an outline of timber. Access to it necessitated building a road from the secondary road which might have been visible from a distance. The view from the living room would have encompassed the town and a ripple of mountain ranges that grew bluer in the distance.

The mayor Hawkeye and the town building committee refused to issue a permit. Price could build a smaller home by the road but the committee would not allow him to deface the hillside he had wanted. Since none of the committee members, most related to each other or to Hawkeye, wanted to talk with him when he called for an explanation, he had no immediate choice but to complain to the town hall receptionist who had nothing by way of insight to offer him.

"This is a picture of my son, Cooper. He's a little older now. And this is my wife. She still looks tired. And we're all eager to move to this area."

"No point in showing me pictures. They mean everything to you. To me, they're just somebody's baby and woman," she said with practiced apathy.

"If they were standing in front of you, crying and wetting?"

"I'd tell them to go home and do it there."

"If they had a home here, that's what they would do."

Although the receptionist gave Price the mayor's special number, he was not helpful. He would not call a special session of the town council to discuss the building permit, as Price had requested. Nor was he was going to put the item on the agenda for discussion at the next regular meeting. Even the threat of legal proceedings did not move him. He had written the bylaws himself.

Price had no other avenue available except to announce he was going to sponsor the building of the town's first senior citizens' center, and leave the naming of it to the mayor. The mayor was very partial to naming an institution after his father or himself. The park already bore his grandmother's name, Flora, which he said really meant a flower, and the intention was to fill up the park with flowers. It had a ragged baseball diamond and a few tulip bulbs at the entrance which flowered until the squirrels would eat off the petals.

The mayor met him for lunch in the only semi-formal dining restaurant on the main street to plan the details of the project and magically handed Price the permit for his house. He also gave Price a copy of the construction bylaws which set out the detailed dos and don'ts of building in the area.

"I highlighted the stuff your contractor should watch out for."

As Price flipped through the bylaw pamphlet, he noticed uneven underlining and asterisks throughout the text. The scribbling irritated him as a defaced wall would. He stared at one aggressive checkmark in the corner of a page, simply saluting the page number and having no other function. Hawkeye had ordered meat and beans.

"You plan it, you stock it, you maintain it, Mr. Mayor."

The mayor said he had served the town for twenty-five years and was intending to retire by the end of the year to follow a career importing high-end purses from Korea.

"Is there a dead city official we can name it after?" Price asked.

"I'm not dead yet."

Hawkeye's brother used to sit on council. Then he started doing well in baggage and accessories and became increasingly insistent that Hawkeye finally hang up the keys to the city. He wanted to expand into designer-type items, especially handbags, but needed a partner he could trust. The mayor was ideal: he knew the per-foot cost of repainting the white line down streets, of budgeting for fifty different items over a year's period. He could judge character without speaking to the man. His best skill was negotiating. Hawkeye's major problem was that he had never traveled overseas nor farther than Florida. There was never any need to go beyond his limits: the world was either the same or in worse condition.

One month later, when the two bulldozers started plowing a road through the forest, a group of fifteen protesters carrying picket signs denouncing the town council; and Price blocked their path by stringing up barbed wire between the trees at the height of the cab of the bulldozer drivers, and standing with arms linked. The confrontation went on for three hours before the local police came out. The igniting of the police cruiser made small headlines in the city newspapers, yet big enough to invite carloads of ecologists to the scene. Sixty protesters warranted a greater police presence although no arrests were immediately made.

As the days became a week, Chazy despaired that the schedule of building contractors would have to be scrapped. Any thought of delivering supplies or breaking ground froze once a van followed by two press vehicles pulled up at the growing media event.

The van driver stepped out, plugged his bullhorn into a wire under the hood and announced:

"My name is Trix. Trees are people too!" The group of passengers traveling in the back of the van let out the appropriate yips as they stretched.

While the protest festered, Price had his building crew use an abandoned logging road at the back of the property, and make their way using all-terrain vehicles carrying materials to the promontory where they built the foundation, frame and installed utilities in a record nine days without alerting the protesters. Trix's van driver was the one whose eye caught the glint of light off the large front window pane almost half a mile away. Some of his cohorts ran into the woods in the general direction of the house. One of them received a fine slash across the eyelid and cheek from the protruding finger of a desiccated birch tree. All of them lost their direction and stopped to argue as the sun began to set in the damp woods.

Even Napanee came to see the new house on the mountain top. Driving up with Cheryl unannounced, she left the car running just as the road reached the semi-circular driveway scalloped out of a thin stand of trees in front of the house. Cheryl remained in the passenger seat fiddling with the radio and assumed her friend momentarily would be returning because there were no other cars parked near the house.

Napanee pushed open the front door which was unlocked. To her surprise, a toddler dressed in nothing but a diaper stood facing her, fifteen feet into the vestibule. He was blond, a slightly inflated belly-button decorated his protruding abdomen and he held an orange tennis ball in his left hand. When he saw her, he looked down, started to swing his arms, looked up again, and weakly threw the ball toward her in an unpracticed underhand.

Chazy came out of the kitchen holding a bib she intended to tie onto the toddler. Both women were startled when they caught sight of each other.

"Chazy…"

"Napanee… I didn't know… It's so good to see you. Come in. Close the door. Are you here alone?"

"Hi, how are you? Cheryl's in the car. I just came by for a minute. Is this your boy?"

"This is Cooper, your grandson," Chazy said as she picked up the child. "Let's go to the kitchen. You can feed him his lunch, if you want."

Napanee stared at the child as if it were a furniture accessory come alive.

"I can't stay… unless I get Cheryl in here."

Carrying Cooper, Chazy walked passed her and out of the house to wave Cheryl in.

"Let's all have lunch. The baby will think it's a party in his honour."

"What's his name again? My cell phone was vibrating in my purse."

Chazy spoke slowly, as if English was not her mother-in-law's first language: "His name is Cooper. The last time you saw him was when he was two months old, sleeping in his crib."

"I knew he would grow up to look like this."

"He looks like you, actually. Same nose and eyes, I think. I often tell that to Price. Doesn't look at all like him."

Cheryl finally entered the house and handed Napanee the car keys. When she saw Cooper, she asked,

"Whose baby is that?"

"Whose do you think it is, Cheryl? Doesn't he look like Chazy?" Napanee said. "Don't you have an alarm system? Anyone can come up this road. You're so isolated."

Chazy told her there were cameras along the road and path. The system was down for the past week. During the tour of the house, the preparation of lunch, the looking at photographs, Chazy could not get Napanee to hold Cooper.

"I want to hug him, Chazy, but he looks like he's soiled."

That was Cheryl's cue for remarking on the flies in the house. She had never seen a fly-paper strip before eyeing the bug-dotted one hanging above the kitchen door.

One gas station consistently posted a gas price two cents higher at the other end of the main street. One, though, sold nothing but gas and garage services, while the other had a franchise snack shop featuring racks of chips, donuts and drinks. Between the two, the ma-and-pa shops flourished during the ski and summer seasons, and toned down in late fall and early spring.

Price walked Main Street hundreds of times and bought extensively at the shops in order to glad-hand people before the elections. Hawkeye told him there was no need to because he was going to win by acclamation, and that voter turn-out was traditionally low.

The experience was invaluable. In City Hall Square, he noticed a skinny-legged boy wiping his dog's lips with the bottom of his T-shirt, and then kiss it. In the regional high school parking lot, a circle of mothers had entangled the wheels of their strollers. They gently pulled and rocked the strollers for minutes, as if they were performing a group dance. Outside the soft ice cream service window of the restaurant, two seagulls yakked about the vanilla debris and pieces of cone they had just swallowed.

The election was held. Price was elected by acclamation, as were all of the councilors. A day before the closing of nominations, Trix managed to file his papers for the position of council member. The mayor Hawkeye told the town clerk to tear up Trix's papers because he was not a resident, tenant or property owner. The clerk called Trix before following his orders. Trix told him he had signed a long-term lease for his van at a local trailer park, which qualified him as a tenant. Although Hawkeye instructed him to destroy the papers, the clerk said he would raise the matter once the new mayor was installed. Price agreed with the process, even going so far as to send Trix and email welcoming the challenge.

At the first meeting of council, Price welcomed the members, and asked Trix to remove his knees from the side of the conference table.

"Mr. Mayor, I was elected to put my knees up. That's what the people want."

"The bylaws do not permit council members to use town property for personal purposes. There is no public purpose served by having your knees shake the table," said Price.

"My people don't want me to put down my knees, Mr. Mayor. Are you going to punch me in the nose?"

Price said no, and put his feet on the table. He asked the others to join him in relaxing if they felt inclined.

The two township policemen, even in two vehicles, were unable to stop the nightly drag racing down the main street after midnight: too many kids, too many cars; and because the municipal judge once threw out a case on a technicality – no such offence as drag-racing - no seventeen year old felt obliged to restrict his driving speed or his proximity to the next car during the starlit events.

Since most of the participants drove souped-up vehicles made in the early 90s, Price had city council pass a bylaw prohibiting the driving of cars manufactured before the year 2000 after 11:00 p.m. on city streets, and permitting the police to impound. The next week, the garage man hauled away one of the dragster's cars which had been conveniently parked at the edge of the family driveway after an evening excursion down Main Street. The teenager's father was so insulted by the heavy-handedness of council that he testified before the judge his son needed the car to bring his enfeebled grandmother to the regional hospital twice a week for dialysis and that his basic liberties were under attack. The judge, again technically-minded, declared the bylaw inapplicable because while the defendant's car was manufactured in 1993, its newer engine, wheels and seats had been manufactured and installed after the year 2000. Besides, one of the police cars was a 1999 model.

On hearing of the decision, Price was tempted to call the judge for a discussion on civic order. After speaking with his lawyer, he decided on a better course of action. That night, Price had the council pass a bylaw reducing the speed limit down Main Street to ten miles per hour, and changing the direction of traffic along the street exactly where dragsters would begin to seriously accelerate, after midnight. Within days, the same judge held that a teenager caught by police going ninety miles per hour in the prohibited direction was not guilty of the charge because the posted signs read "after 12 am" without specifying at what time the prohibition ceased. He ruled that because the time period made no sense, neither did the prohibition.

Price then told council it had no choice but to pass a curfew bylaw, permitting police to arrest any person under the age of nineteen found in the streets, parks or other public places after 11 p.m. Two councilors voted against, two for, with Price breaking the tie in favour of passage of the law.

The first teenager to receive a ticket for curfew violation was Janice Koho, who had to walk around the block several times to deal with a panic attack. When the police officer warned her from his car to get back home, she kept walking briskly, her eyes looking downward and focused on anything unusual within seven feet to her left or right. The officer chased her to her house, where he caught up with her on the porch. Mr. Koho tried to straighten out the situation for his daughter. The officer told him to complain to the Mayor.

At municipal court the next week, her father pleaded not guilty on account of a panic attack. In addition, he told the judge that since having been chased through the streets and getting a ticket for two hundred dollars, his daughter had refused to go out of the house and stopped being ambidextrous.

"She's sixteen, Your Honour. All her life we made sure she painted with two hands, wrote with her left and right and she was perfectly coordinated. The whole week, she's been doing watercolour with only her right hand. Janice refused to use her left when typing at the computer. At the piano, she's just pecking with her right forefinger."

"What do you think happened, Mr. Koho?" the judge asked.

"She thinks one side of her died because of being so frightened. She says her left side is out to get her," he answered from the accused's bar.

"Has this happened before?"

"When she was much younger and throwing tantrums when we held one arm behind her back to get her used to switching."

The judge held that it was not necessary to register a not-guilty plea since there was no offense. The City does not have the jurisdiction to create age-based curfews. Twenty-four other accuseds present for their pleas that day rose yelping with excitement, including the seventeen year old organizer of the drag races. He had received six tickets which the judge, surprisingly, upheld, saying that the offender was the only one whom the bylaw legitimately targeted.

Chazy did not want to hear herself say the words. She could not control herself.

"Cooper's been kidnapped. Come home right away. He's gone," she sobbed into the telephone.

Price ran into the bingo hall where he organized a search party. He immediately raised thirty people and twenty vehicles.

Police found no note, no message. They had dogs with them. Five inspectors, seven uniforms, each carrying on a different conversation on their phones. Chazy had put Cooper to sleep right after Napanee and Cheryl left. She had also napped. When she awoke and went to check on him, he was gone. Maybe he had wandered off into the woods. Maybe the front door had been left ajar. Which was worse: a toddler alone in the woods wearing only a diaper and night shirt, or being taken by a stranger?

Price suspected foul play by Trix, by Harry, by a few investment applicants he had turned down. It could have been one or two people in town who had expressed animosity over the past few months. He thought it would be helpful to prepare a list of suspects for police, and for himself. He wrote down ten names, then fifteen, and, ultimately, thirty-five. Price stopped to consider who he noted as untrustworthy or even criminally inclined as a result of hostility he had attracted. These constituted the dark side of the world he enjoyed. How much longer would the list be if he lived in another country where enmity and tribalism had been sanctioned by law throughout its cultural history? He was living in a society which he felt had reached the highest level of social development, and as a result gave him the comfort, even in a moment of fear, that there were ways of dealing swiftly with this blackness. Price printed the names, numbers and other information about the individuals on his dark list off his computer for the police inspector. He was surprised at his organization, to the extent that it immediately aroused his suspicion about Price's own involvement.

"Officer, I am a young wealthy white person residing in an isolated community. I have views which I think are right and forceful, and with which others do not agree. I know certain people wish me and my family harm, and I keep a list for eventualities. There are many others I do not know, and so I take precautions," Price explained.

The inspector told him his son could have simply wandered out into the forest.

"The forest may be your biggest enemy."

Four hours after Chazy had first called to report the kid-napping, Napanee and Cheryl drove up to Price's house where they saw pick-up trucks lining the upper part of the road and police cruisers filling the driveway and parking area. They were stopped by a policeman within view of the house.

"What's going on? My son is Price DeMann. He lives in there and I have his son in my back seat", Napanee protested.

At the policeman's beckoning, a number of officers gathered around her car. Napanee spotted Chazy in front of the house.

"Chazy, Chazy, over here. What's happening? Do you want your son?"

They had taken him shopping.

Days after Price and his family returned to the city, he received a call from the town fire chief, second cousin to Hawkeye.

"Burnt clear down to the ground. A few window panes standing, cracked. Burnt clear down."

"What are you saying, Chief?" Price asked, genuinely won-dering what he was talking about.

"Your house. Just a big camp fire now. Sprinklers were no good."

"How did it happen?" Price was stunned.

"Don't know, except for the soda bottles of gasoline. Wasn't yours, was it?" the Chief asked. "Burnt a hole in the top of the mountain. A lot of trees gone."

"Arson. Are you saying someone burned it down?"

"Didn't have to. Looks like a few bad people hauled some bottles up and threw them. Like the cocktails."

"Molotov cocktails? Someone threw gasoline at the house?"

"Better come up here. See for yourself. Total loss, down to the ground." The Chief had exhausted his powers of descrip-tion, and hung up.

Chazy's first thought was of the baby accessories all over the house, which were now gone if the Chief's report was true. She urged Price to call him back to get more details. He called the insurance agency, then immediately set out to see it for himself. On the way, he picked up an email forwarded by Chazy, originally from Trix, which simply said: "Condolences." She saved it for the police.

At the entrance of the mountain road, Price drove past a group of hecklers bearing signs reading "Too bad" and "On Top of Old Smokey".

When he reached the remains of his home, he was stopped from leaving his car by a policeman.

"That's my house, Sir."

"The policeman told him they had found a body nearby, probably that of an arsonist, burnt beyond recognition, his abdomen covered with molten plastic, probably a container carrying the gasoline used to set the fire.

Price had never thought of Trix as evil. Evil required an on-going intelligent commitment, not to chaos, but to opposing good intention. Trix was simply an extreme contrarian, a prince in opposition to life and family. He was more than a common criminal, more than a delinquent because he needed masses of people to use for his asocial ends.

Had he been any better at organization, Trix would have succeeded in killing Price's wife and child. When Price had learned of his death, he had the same feeling he experienced when picking through the dead enemy outside the caves. The dead were simply not smart enough, their cause not sufficiently clear to give them any greater skill in surviving. Rather than driving home a point, dying was the admission by an amateur of failure of cause and process.

Chapter 17

They See The Meaning of Life

The restaurant looked deceptively ordinary for a crucible of faith: six tables, under lit, a family business, generous portions, a storefront looking out on a limited number of pedestrians. It was not Harry's favorite place because at night, the lighting was too dim to permit him to read his magazine.

That evening he did not want to read, only eat. Since he was tired of life, he concluded, he ordered a large plate of very crisp chicken wings. He told the waiter, long-haired, thin, eager to make it through university, that he did not want to find turkey wings mixed into his serving.

While he waited, steeping his hunger with intense melancholy, he noticed he was the sole customer in the restaurant. Maybe he was early; maybe the clientele knew something he did not. He then noticed he was alone in the universe.

Before a stab of panic could strike him, the waiter brought the food which smelled crisp. That delightful sense was good enough to bring Harry back to his goal that evening. Using his fingers, he immediately pulled apart the first hot portion of wings, pulling the meat from the brittle bones and skin, then eating the skin. His fingers delighted in the fresh grease. The chicken was his reward for solitude, for the lack of recognition by his own son, by the women he had known, or his immense need to change society to suit his image.

When he was full, he looked around for a napkin. The waiter, who had been watching him, quickly approached and asked him not to clean his hands on the newly ironed tablecloth.

"Where are the napkins?"

"We don't have any. But you can wipe your fingers in my hair, I have specially long hair that is dry."

Harry thought it was a generous gesture. He grabbed his hair as the waiter bent down, and found the grease quickly lifted from his fingers from pulling on the strands. Harry left him a larger than usual tip.

It was the way the waiter said "Thank you". That was humanity expressing gratitude. Harry was so overwhelmed, he asked if he could sit at the table a little while longer before leaving, even if he was not interested in dessert. At that very table, he saw the meaning of life, which he resolved to do something about. He would preach it to whomever would listen, and once a month, come back to the same spot to renew the revelation.

Having had his revelation, Harry was ready to purify his soul. Only for that reason did he find himself in the cemetery looking for his father's gravestone. He had no idea where it was because he had not gone to his father's funeral when he died four years before. The name of the cemetery came up on an internet search.

Harry had explained to his mother:

"I wanted to come. I even bought a new hat, a black serious hat."

"Where were you?"

"It was windy. The hat wouldn't stay on my head. I couldn't show up without it."

"You never wear a hat, Harry."

"What if I were standing at the grave and the wind blew my hat right into the pit, right on top of the coffin. Who would go get it? Would they just shovel dirt over it and bury dad with my hat somewhere in his dirt. It doesn't make sense.

The day was sunny enough for a picnic. The burial society office gave him a map of graves to follow, which brought him to a line of gravestones. From the path, he could see a family had gathered at a location very close to where his father supposedly lay. His brief confident speech to his father asking forgiveness quickly evaporated in the fear that the family was his family.

He pulled the peak of his baseball cap lower over his face and kept walking a safe distance where he would be beyond recognition. Behind a gravestone engraved with the name "Silverdigger", he squinted at the father, mother and two children standing and gesticulating at a site. What gave them away was the groomed skunk on a leash. Harry knew no relatives with a skunk, and so concluded it was safe to approach.

His father's stone was immediately next to where the family was gathered. They glanced at each other, confirming they had no mutual business. The skunk barked at Harry, bared its teeth and coughed until slapped by one of the children. Realizing coughing was not acceptable, the animal lunged at Harry's leg, causing him reflexively to move out of the line of attack. Its teeth caught the cuff of his pants, making a small, ragged rip.

The commotion was not what Harry had expected. The obvious occurred to him. His father was still angry at him for his neglect. The dead spoke through the skunk. Had his father been alive, he would have wanted to hit him. Instead, he tried to bite him. The family was a pack of angels bent on doing him ill. Harry stepped back, even though the mother approached him with extended arms to express an apology. Harry walked briskly away, breaking into a run when the skunk resumed coughing.

In order to focus on the core value of life, Harry realized his work time should reflect his philosophy. He bought a store that sold only darts and dart boards. He bought it for next to nothing because the owner had lost interest in the sport and was now interested in importing aromatic coffees. In the back, Harry found racks of dart boards made of wood, cork, plastic and blends. Most were bulls-eye patterned, some checkered, others striped. A few had angry animal faces.

Harry the Dartman showed customers at least ten times a day how to concentrate on the target, a poor metaphor for the ultimate goal of life, how to balance the dart, respect its tip, care for its wings. One man with two parts in his hair said dart throwing was like curling when it came to putting the thrower into the animus of the thrown. Without losing his temper, Harry said the two ports were parallel galaxies, curling having lost its dominance once all its stars burnt out. In the end, there was no dispute, the curler being so poor at throwing darts, he was liable to injure the wall and himself.

The business permitted Harry to live his new dogma, even though he had not sold one complete set since he opened. Impulse-buying would not bring a spate of sales. Neither would championship players who would create their own darts and repair their own boards after long hours of patient practice. His spirit, driven by pure lucidity, found the solution. Darts and pizza. Harry simply micro-waved store-bought frozen pizza and sprayed the shop with spice-tinged air freshener. He closed after a run of two months, after a basement flood dev-astated the inventory and the insurer agreed to pay the retail value of what had been damaged and what might not have been there at all.

Harry called Cheryl at the office. She hung up twice without bothering to respond to him. The third time he called, she blurted out:

"Why are you calling. Are you taping this conversation?"

"I'll talk for one minute. You don't have to say anything. So even if I'm taping, I'm only taping myself, okay?"

Cheryl rose to pace. She agreed with the logic he proposed. Since he was not sure he had snagged her, he asked if she was still on the line. She tapped the phone with her index fingernail.

"I know Napanee is looking for a lot of investment money. I can get it for her. No charge. From Price. She wants it from Price, I can get it from him. Legit. No fee."

Cheryl tapped on the phone again.

"I am a newly born person. For years I was lost in self-ishness and nothing but helping myself. I don't have to do that anymore. Tell Napanee I want to fix things for us. IF she says no, I'll accept her wishes. No harm done. I'll call again tomorrow at this time."

Cheryl hung up without having said a word. She caught Napanee in her office, pulling a fluff ball from her sweater. When Cheryl told her about Harry's call, Napanee was strangely magnanimous.

"If and when he calls tomorrow, tell him I'll meet him at the largest hotel lobby in the city at 5."

When Harry called, Cheryl gave him explicit instructions.

"Wear a jogging outfit. An old one. On your feet, running shoes. I mean dirty and beat-up running shoes. On your head, a baseball cap, sort of faded. Nothing new. If you wear anything new, no meeting. Casual is the rule, no chic, understand? Make a hole in the knee of your pants. Which knee doesn't matter."

Napanee found him reading a newspaper on the oversized fauteuil closest to the reception desk. Generous, deep-green potted open fans of ferns provided a border at each end of the sitting area. The multiple columns majestically defined the lobby, their capitols gilded with thick metallic daubs. The commotion of guests dragging personal baggage on wheels, huddles of conference attendees in lapel name tags, uniformed porters waiting for assignments, sporadic pacers and wall leaners could not make enough noise to withstand the muffle imposed by the smart design of the place. No one could shout loud enough to impress or alert.

Cheryl had done a walk-by minutes before to see if Harry had conformed to instructions. She saw a bell captain approach him, presumably to find out what he was doing there.

Napanee took a seat one couch-cushion away from him.

"You look like you live in a dumpster, Harry."

Harry stood up long enough to have Napanee wave him back to his seated position. Her lavender-jasmine perfume overpowered the lobby evergreen scent. Her sequined powder blue evening dress just covered her collar bones and revealed her scapulas in the back. A matching laced scarf curved loosely under the base of her neck. She was dressed for an evening occasion which was not taking place.

Harry slowly realized he had been set up at a disadvantage.

"I don't know if I recognize you. What's your proposal?"

"You look..." Harry started to say.

"There's no time for anything except your proposal," she interrupted.

"Short and sweet. Our son never had parents, together. We're his parents. We finally get together. We show Price we have intentions. A big reunion party. Our son is so eager for our re-match to work, Harry throws some money our way."

Napanee had been looking at the pattern in the extensive rug at her feet. She finally stared at him.

"Is that your big idea? What sort of money are you expecting?"

"Nothing. Absolutely nothing. I read the article on your business in the paper. It said you needed investment to expand. I figured if your own son had money, and you needed it, then he wasn't giving it to you for a reason. Believe me, I'm a new man," he said, trying to avoid staring at Napanee's truly impressive make-up and outfit.

"Since when?" she asked.

"Since I saw the meaning of life at a restaurant." Harry confessed.

"Cheryl has your phone number. Goodbye."

She walked straight toward the bell captain, who had been watching them from his stand about forty feet away. As soon as he heard her say Harry smelled and had made an immoral remark to her, he accompanied by his assistants, strode toward Harry, caught him by the elbows and rushed him out of the hotel as if he were soiled laundry.

Chazy found herself on the party committee with Cheryl. When she first learned of the Harry-Napanee reunion plans, she warned Price that a maneuver was underway. She did not realize the impact the party was having on her husband until he told her.

"It's a good thing, isn't it?" Price said as they dressed for the event.

Chazy chose her words carefully.

"It should be. Parents coming together should be a blessing."

"But is it Chazy?"

"I have never said anything untruthfully negative about either of them, have I?"

"No."

"If they're doing it for themselves, who am I to throw cold water on them. If this is something to do with making you act against your will or better judgment, I have a big problem."

The party hall was next door to a wedding reception. Some of the wedding guests wandered innocently into the party, oblivious to the wrong context, and ate off the smorgasbord. Napanee personally approved the dozen man-sized, silk-screened hearts standing in the corners and sides of the hall. The cloth napkins had a gold point of the names of the hosts, Napanee's name overwhelming Harry's in size. The twelve piece band was mainly brass, brokering 1950s music led at crucial moments by a sleepy saxophone. The two hundred guests were mainly Napanee's office workers, suppliers, bankers and professionals.

Harry sat at a mock head table hemmed in by two men wearing shiny tuxedos, the wing-tips at the top of their ruffled shirts peeking out of their meaty chins like incisors. Whenever he shifted in his chair, his companions turned their heads toward him like slow mechanical dolls do, leaving him with a menace of ill consequences in the event he actually stood up. At one point, he told the guard on his right:

"You know, it's my party. That's my picture up there on the screen."

The guard did not acknowledge hearing him, nor understanding the same language.

"What if I were to scream my head off from this chair?"

The other guard's slow head swiveled toward him. Harry recorded his resignation by announcing he was going to lean forward to grasp the salad dressing hiding behind the floral table centerpiece.

After a trite introduction by Cheryl, Napanee placed herself behind the podium on the bandstand to explain the evening. Without once looking at Harry, she spoke longingly about returning to the good times, and overlooking the problems.

"I and Harry have matured. Our view of life has finally overlapped. I can't say we see eye to eye on everything. I do know we agree that family once, family always. So we decided to do this in stages. We're going to date. Harry's agreed to act as a consultant to my business. Who knows what will happen after that. With the support and encouragement of our family and friends, the best is yet to come."

Cheryl coaxed Chazy to bring her son up to Napanee, who swept him up, air-kissed his cheek and briskly put him down. The child lost his breath but quickly wound up his throat to wail. The clapping and cheers drowned him out. The applause sounded both heartfelt and contrived. Balloons were released from a ceiling net. The band smartly interwove Here Comes The Bride with Those Were The Days. A brigade of waitresses fanned out with trays of Irish Coffee and Chocolate Mousse.

By the third week after the party, Napanee could not wait any longer. She let the roots of her hair show. Instead of the business suit she usually wore, she acquired an ill-fitting blouse with a floral pattern and a mismatched discount skirt that showed wrinkles. The tennis shoes she had not worn for years and an outstretched bra completed her outfit.

"Price, I brought you some muffins. No grease, just a little oil. Still warm."

"How's your partner?"

"You mean your father. He's a wonderful man. Completely different person. And we both want to make it work."

"You're certainly putting in a lot of effort."

"I want it for our family. Want to taste a muffin? Low on sugar. Price, one of the ways Harry and I want to cement our relationship is by working together. He has a street sense of business, and I have the consistency. All we need is an investment to boost us forward."

"You're looking to family money. My money."

"Of course, dear. It's to keep our family together."

"How much?"

"I still need eighteen million. If you put in half, I can get the rest from other sources."

Price looked closely at her outfit. He had never seen her mismatched. The scent of muffins pervaded the area around his desk.

Napanee had no need for books, except for romance novels. Romance was a sign that people were alert about what they could get from others. It was not the falling-in-love that was of any interest to her: what people did with their love could rivet her for five hundred pages. She skipped Eros, the sap, the description of magnetism. Her reading astuteness permitted her to get to the core of what she wanted to spend her time on: how a couple went on to build an empire, how one spouse became an addict or a criminal deviant while the other had no clue, how the marriage brought shame or guilt, or conflict, or even happiness to the extended families. Napanee never read biographies because she knew they were not true. Autobiographies, of course, were pure fiction. Most of these dealt with sexual conquest or political achievement, which were as interesting to her as learning Urdu.

"Cheryl, I'm going to pull down the Library. There are still books in there. Why don't you go through them and see if you want anything."

Cheryl declined, suggesting most of the inventory was probably riddled with mould or real book worms.

"It was a kid's library, wasn't it?"

"An everything library. Maybe a hundred years old. You're right. The wrecker will just mush everything into the ground."

Later, though, it struck Cheryl that the building might contain money or special books which might have value. She telephoned Napanee to tell her she would go in with someone from the wreckers to look around. She would need huge lights and gloves and maybe a pellet gun if she encountered any danger.

On the appointed morning, she met an intoning wrecker who gave her a hard hat, an industrial floodlight, an air mask and steel-toed boots before they entered. Cheryl brought her own shopping bags to cart away valuables.

After one hour, they salvaged scores of classic comics, several in almost mint condition. Most were scattered around the reading rooms under chairs or behind the iron radiators. The real treasure was located in a locked closet in the basement which the wrecker forced open by smashing off the door handle with an iron pipe he found on the floor. Inside, Cheryl found stacks of fountain pens, erasers and scrap books which she eagerly shoved into her shopping bags.

On the shelves built into the closet, the wrecker picked a volume out of the rows of books. It contained an undated note written on card paper, which said simply: *"To the Ketchums... Dickens."* Other signatures he located either inside book covers or on book marks on cards in a small wooden letter box were those reading Frost, Zola, Crane, Wells, Thoreau, Wilder or Verne.

"Want any of this junk?" he asked.

"What is it?"

"Looks like stuff from library members," he said.

"There's a smell in here. What am I breathing?"

"Dust, mould. I gave you a mask."

She said it would smudge her lipstick.

"I have what I need. The rest goes down with the building. Unless you and your friends want to take all these copies of the Bobsy Twins," she said. As she stepped back, she though something fell to the closet floor where she detected some movement. When the wrecker shone the light downward, they saw a young raccoon with glassy eyes, one paw raised.

Cheryl shrieked.

"It's not a rat, lady," the wrecker said as he approached the animal.

"If it's not a rat, it must have rat friends living in the walls," she said. She threw away her shopping bags, fearing the items she had placed inside might have been touched by animal feces.

"Tear it all down," Cheryl said as they emerged on the first floor.

After she left in her car, the wrecker stayed behind. In fact, he stayed the whole night, searching through all the possible hidden closets and chests, recovering exquisite artifacts which he placed in his rare book store, open only on weekends.

Price looked at Napanee as if he had reflected on the proposal for a long time. The anticipation of getting something out of her son had left her tired at this moment. Maybe that was the way to appear, fatigued with life, counting on a token of appreciation that should have meant more to the son than the mother.

"Why should you have to scrounge. Mom, you were right from the beginning. You need the money, you should get it. Now that you brought Harry back in the picture, everything is complete. I couldn't be happier to be your main investor. Everything I have I owe to you anyway."

As he spoke, Napanee rose then quietly deflated.

"I'm going to put the money in a trust. Harry will be the trustee, and he'll distribute the funds when he thinks it's right to any of your investment companies. We keep the trust and the companies separate for tax reasons. A real Chinese Wall between them. Whenever you're ready for the funds, all you have to do is ask Harry to disburse. Once I put the money into the trust, I have no further control. That way, it's between you and him."

She did not know what to say.

"You're putting eighteen million dollars into Harry's hands?"

That's the only way it'll work."

"But… what if…"

"That's between you and Harry. Since you're life partners, he'll write the cheques, and really add something to your business."

"You don't understand. If you put money, especially that much money, into Harry's hands, it ain't goin' nowhere but his own pocket. We'll never see it again."

Price tried to look impatient with her.

"I'm basing myself on tax and legal advice. Keep the two entities separate, no interlocking control."

"Harry doesn't have to be involved. Put one of my people in charge of the trust. Put your lawyer in charge."

"That misses the point. I want us to be a family again. You came up with a great idea. That family that works together…"

"I didn't mean it that way."

"Either Harry is part of the investment plan, or there is no investment. That's the way my advisors put it."

"Well, tell them there is no Harry."

"You know what that means."

Napanee stared at her son as if she were dealing with a difficult supplier. This supplier saw through the sales talk. Rather than admitting a check-mate, she was proud he was endowed with her ability to confront, demand and withhold.

"I give up, Price. I don't want you to lose your money. Forget about it. I'll get it another way."

Harry called Cheryl to find out what the next move was. He told her he remembered Napanee's promise to find him an office, and start paying within a few weeks.

"No, Harry. No one promised anything. No one said anything about a few weeks."

"I know what I heard."

"There is a message from Napanee, though. I want you to write this down so you won't forget. Got a pen?"

"Go ahead."

"The message is "Drop dead." If you call again, the police will take you away."

Harry took the news of his ouster as would an inspector on a conveyor belt take the next dirty bottle. He was not surprised, but he was interested. No explanation was given, nor was one requested.

His tranquility arose from his preoccupation with his own digit. Accidentally, he had slammed a drawer on his thumb, causing his nail to bleed. Once the pain was gone and several days had passed, he noticed a miniature portrait configured by grooves in his thumbnail and congealed streaks of blood had formed in his cuticle. At first, it looked like his father;

then it looked like himself. It was a sign. His hand held his essence. Harry was what he accomplished by his actions, not his thoughts. Literally at the tip of his fingers, he had proof of the existence of his own soul.

He took a picture of his thumbnail. The portrait was out of focus and disappeared after the flash.

Chapter 18

The Library

All that was needed to demolish the Library was a backhoe with a front-end shovel. The arm broke through the windows and surrounding wall, which caused the roof to collapse. Since the building was flat-roofed, it was fairly easy to implode the structure. The claw chewed away at the floors as the dust and smell of wall-interiors wafted upward.

Napanee had two cameras on tripods rolling to capture the demolition. A crowd swelled, receded and swelled again beyond the orange construction tape bordering the site.

"I'll buy all the piping and radiators. It's cast iron. Don't throw it away," pestered a neatly dressed man after he emerged from a convertible. He pulled a wallet from his back pocket to which was stuck the corner of a wrinkled handkerchief.

Napanee asked for an offer in writing.

"Lady, all the junk is going into the dumpster as we're talking. If I don't cart it away now, it's junk. No one's going to go fishing through the bricks and cement for it."

She took five hundred dollars in cash for dozens of radiators and the huge basement furnace. She only got fifty dollars for the wiring. The scrap iron buyer spoke loudly on his car phone to a trucker who was not willing to come down immediately to do a pick-up. He then spoke something softly into the phone, waited and smiled. The trucker would come right away after all, not as a personal favour, but as a matter of coercion.

"He's my student," the buyer told Napanee, who showed no interest, except when he said that it's always good to know a trucker.

"You know, you're right. Like for emergencies," she echoed.

"I taught him philosophy in jail for university credit. I was paroled before he handed in his final paper. He's still working on it."

"Give me his name and number," she said, handing him a miniature pen and slip of paper.

"Patterns of speech used by teenagers in the 50s. Good topic."

Once the site was flattened and the cavity filled in, she posted a for sale sign on a huge placard buttressed by two-by-fours. The sign was the closing image on the video cassette which she sent by messenger to Price, with a card that read: *"This is what you wanted. Call me if you want to buy the land."*

Price watched the video with fascination, not emotion. He had known the inside, not the outside of the Library. Those images of the interior of the first floor exposed by the collapse of the external wall were too fleeting to absorb. There was no book bin against the southern wall: either it had fallen into the ruin or it had been moved out prior to the demolition. Price suspected his mother had removed the carpeted bathtub for storage and ransom. That is what she had wanted him to see.

About the Author

Lazar Sarna currently writes and lectures on literary and professional issues, and practices law in Montreal Canada. He is the author of the poetry collections He Claims He is the Heir and Letters of State, both through Porcupine's Quill, as well as the novels The Man Who Lived Near Nelligan, Coach House Press and Book Bin Baby, Adelaide Books. His poetry has appeared in Antigonish Review, Canadian Forum, Canadian Literature, Descant, Fiddlehead, and Prism International. The poetry book He Claims He is the Heir was nominated as finalist for the Quebec Writers Federation Award.

Sarna has lectured at the McGill University Law Faculty, and the John Molson School of Business at Concordia University. As a member of the Quebec Bar Association, he has addressed professional credit conferences and pleaded before most court jurisdictions including the Supreme Court of Canada. His numerous legal publications are frequently cited by the courts in Canada.

Thematically, Sarna's poetry veers toward the edge of the believable, gaining the reader's initial trust that what he is dealing was actually experienced. Common apprehensions, mildewing institutions, and faded love are carefully managed, reheated into a satisfying meal.

It is no secret that unique, strange and complex stories that come though the office of a lawyer form an inspirational source of poetry. The tantalizing ability to mind other people's business gives Sarna a head start in the race to capture a realistic yet imaginary world otherwise unseen. The Tethered Man is rooted in ancient sources, but comes alive through the painful humour of people we should know better. As titular head of a large and growing family, he is also blessed with a built-in audience.

Made in the USA
Monee, IL
20 February 2020